THE
CIRCLE
OF THE
EARTH

Asher looks around the room, and he cannot tell if everyone is backing Moates, or not. Who knows what has been said, and to whom? Asher feels suddenly very alone.

"This just ain't the way things ought to be," Asher says.

"You need to put away childish things," Moates replies. "This is the way the great world turns. This is the way things *are*. Big difference between *is* and *ought*. Always has been. Always will be."

"Not *always* will be," Asher says. "And anyway, that *ought* comes from somewhere, and I ain't walking all over it, like it ain't even there."

Hymns of Kingdom

*In the immense cathedral which is the universe of God,
each man, whether scholar or manual laborer,
is called to act as the priest of his whole life –
to take all that is human,
and to turn it into an offering and a hymn of glory.*

Paul Evdokimov

www.hymnsofkingdom.com

WILLIAM TICKEL

THE
CIRCLE
OF THE
EARTH

A HYMN OF KINGDOM

VENTRIS & BYWATER

Ventris & Bywater
412 South White Street
Suite 114
Athens, Tennessee 37303
www.ventrisandbywater.com

The Circle of the Earth/William Tickel (1951-   )
ISBN 978-0-9888900-3-9

Back Cover Painting: *Asher's Sunrise* by Lisa Bell
http://www.lisabellfineart.net

Cover Photograph:
"Ferry from Brownsville to Matamoros, 1915"
Courtesy of The Center for American History
The University of Texas at Austin
The Robert Runyon Photograph Collection
[txuruny 02828]

"Hymns of Kingdom" Series Cover designed by Barbara Martin
("Charala" at 99designs.com)

"Hymns of Kingdom" Logo designed by Suzana Vučković
("Suzy Design" at 99designs.com)

This text has been prepared with Adobe InDesign
using Adobe Caslon Pro

2022.03.03

12   11   10   9   8   7   6   5   4   3   2   **1**

DEDICATION

To

Steven Meller

*… for a brief conversation in the aisle
that has charted the course of my dotage.*

Epigraphs

It is he that sitteth upon the circle of the earth,
and the inhabitants thereof *are* as grasshoppers;
that stretcheth out the heavens as a curtain,
and spreadeth them out as a tent to dwell in:

Isaiah 40:22

And the things you can't remember
Tell the things you can't forget
That history puts a saint in every dream.

Tom Waits
"Time"

South Texas
1915

LAREDO, TEXAS
MARCH, 1915

1

Later, when the necessity for accountability becomes unavoidable, a commission of sorts will be formed, and polished men will sit at polished benches and ask polished questions for reasons that have little to do with the pursuit of truth. It will emerge from these hearings, with much reluctance, that Emilio Sanchez was first observed on horseback in Brooks County at mid-morning on Tuesday, March 23rd, riding northward across the flat, dry scrubland, pack mule in tow.

It is a petroleum geologist named Dennison who sees him, a mile across the section he is charting, and he feels faintly unsettled at the interruption of his assumption of solitude. But the sight arouses enough curiosity that he pulls his field glasses from his saddlebag and watches for a few moments as the distant figure moves across his field of vision and then drops from sight into an arroyo.

Dennison puts his glasses away and finishes his readings. By the middle of the afternoon, he has made the three-hour horseback ride north-east, back into Falfurrias, the Brooks County seat. He spends the rest of the day in his rented office, charting his findings for his next report to the Standard Oil Company of New Jersey. He thinks no more of the figure at all until dinner that evening at his boarding house where, during a lull in the conversation, he mentions casually to the others at the table what he has seen.

It surprises him when Chantry, a Brooks County deputy sheriff who has a room down the hall, takes an active interest.

"Mexican?" Chantry asks. "How do you know?"

"Sombrero," Dennison answers. "Posture. I don't know. You just sense it."

"And you're certain there was only the one?"

Dennison considers his reply. The lawman has always seemed distant to him, even arrogant, but it seems that Chantry's interest is coupled with a vague approval of some sort.

"The one's all I saw for sure," Dennison says, but now he hesitates for a moment and then adds the five words that will make everything go so terribly wrong: "There *could* have been more."

Chantry digests this for a spell, while the dinner conversation moves on to other things.

After dessert, Dennison moves to the parlor and settles in for his evening hour with the San Antonio newspaper, unaware, for now, that his casual desire to impress a man he does not like will result in the death of a man he does not know.

Chantry ponders his options for a few moments and then walks three blocks to the County Sheriff's office, on the first floor of the new County Courthouse. It is a brisk evening, and a chill is arriving with the darkness. He finds his boss, a taciturn man named Burgess, filling out the weekly meal requisitions for the county jail.

Chantry waits for Burgess to look up, but the only recognition he receives is a terse, "What?"

Burgess's gruffness makes Chantry suddenly unsure of his desire to raise this issue, but he is committed now and forges ahead. "Fellow at dinner said he saw some greasers on horseback moving north."

The sheriff's gaze rises from the forms. "When, and how many?"

"Couldn't say how many. More than one horse. Pack horses, too. This morning, down near Baluarte Creek."

Burgess considers this. "Probably nothing," he finally says.

"The only reason I mention it is that it seems like they might be headed to San Diego."

Chantry's statement of the obvious irritates Burgess, but he is damned if he will let Chantry see that. "All right," he says, and he returns his attention to the requisitions. Chantry waits for a moment and then returns to his boarding house, unaware, for now, that his casual desire to impress a man he does not like will result in the death of a man he does not know. And so it goes.

Burgess completes the requisitions and puts them to one side, and retrieves from his desk the communication from the Governor's office that has arrived by special courier the week before. He rereads it with careful attention. After a routine arrest in McAllen in early January, a "manifesto" had been found in the pocket of a Mexican national, calling for a general uprising against the Anglo population of south Texas, and the summary execution of all white males over the age of sixteen. This document was supposedly drafted in San Diego, the county seat of Duval County, less than fifty miles north of Falfurrias. Burgess has never reckoned it credible; Archibald Parr controls Duval County, and nothing like that would have gotten past him. To Burgess, it was most likely a bunch of drunken Mexicans leading each other on. The date for the uprising has passed without incident. But folks are nervous, and the Governor is emphatic that the violence occurring south of the Rio Grande must not be allowed to spill northward into south Texas.

Burgess returns the paper to his desk drawer and leans back in his chair, lacing his fingers behind his neck, and deliberates. He has a dilemma. He knows that this is probably nothing, and he understands how much commotion there will be when he raises the alarm. But he has just won a close reelection the previous November. If he ignores this, and it turns out to be something consequential, his career will be over.

Burgess lifts the earpiece from the telephone on his desk, thinks for a moment, and then replaces it in its cradle. Lydia, the night switchboard operator, will almost certainly eavesdrop on any conversation, and it will be all over town within minutes. His instinct also tells him that this communication should be formally on the record.

After a moment, he stands up, reaches for his hat, and walks across the street to the telegraph office.

In the years to come, with the hindsight of known consequence, Burgess will often relive this moment, standing in the Western Union Office: the oversized clock on the back wall; the pad of blank sheets at the counter where he stands, pencil in hand, as he composes the text of the telegram; the darkness outside, unseen in the large reflective window; and the sleepy indifference of the night operator, waiting patiently for the message to be torn off the pad and handed to him. Burgess will imagine himself not leaving his office. He will imagine himself apologizing to the clerk and turning around and leaving the office, telegram unwritten and unsent. He will imagine himself sending the telegram and then almost immediately sending a second telegram canceling the meaning of the first one. He will relive every opportunity he had not to send a communication he felt to be spurious, and he will endure some measure of regret for his part in the result for the rest of his days.

The telegram is sent to Henry Hutchings, the Texas State Adjutant General, who heads the Texas Rangers. Hutchings reads it and considers a prudent course of action. This is all but guaranteed to be of no importance, but he has only recently been appointed by Governor Ferguson, who has just won a close election the previous November. If he ignores this and it turns out to be something consequential, his career will be over. And so it goes.

Company A is headed by Captain Sanders in Del Rio, who cannot effectively coordinate anything from that distance. Captain Fox and his Company B, based in Valentine, is understaffed. Company C is here in Austin and is Captain Smith's one-man investigation unit. That leaves Captain Moates in Laredo, and his Company D. Moates has a man in Alice and a man in Hebbronville. Both are close to Falfurrias.

So he telegraphs Moates and asks him to have someone look into it. He knows Moates and does not fully trust him, so he frames the text of the telegram with great care.

It is now 9:45 on Tuesday night.

Render Moates is in his study at home when his wife informs him that a messenger is asking for him. He walks down the wide hallway to the front vestibule, where he encounters an earnest young man with a telegram in his hand. Moates tips him and moves under the overhead light, and unfolds the yellow page.

His wife watches him read it and sees a familiar, furtive pleasure pass over his face. It is a look that she has seen many times before. It is a look that troubles her thoughts. It is a look that disquiets her sleep. It is a look that she has come to loathe.

"What is it?" she asks.

"Nothing," Moates says. He returns to his den and shuts the door.

Moates makes a single telephone call, and ninety minutes later, he is sitting with his Company Sergeant, Horace Miller, in his mannered and leathered District Office. Its walls are covered with impressive maps, framed prints, and the elegantly mounted heads of elk and buffalo. A large pool table occupies one-fourth of the floor. It is a man's room. Moates has devoted much time and personal expense to having it present a carefully crafted impression of himself.

They both have a glass of whiskey in their hands, poured by Moates personally. For Miller, it is either way too late or way too early to be imbibing, but he says nothing and dutifully sips.

"I am sorry to call you in on short notice like this," Moates is saying. He hands Miller the telegram and regards him as he reads it. He watches Miller's face change from curious to perplexed. Moates has the same questions in his mind that he expects Miller to raise, but Moates also has something that Miller does not: the ability to recognize a political advantage when it lands in his lap.

"This is very vague," Miller says.

"I think there's something to it," Moates responds. "If Hutchings thought it was vague, it would have never been sent." Moates swivels in his chair and turns to a large map of Texas mounted on the wall behind his desk. There is a pool cue leaning against the wall under the map, and Moates reaches for it. Miller cannot help but note that the cue is a prop, placed there before the curtain rose on this particular act of the drama. Everything Moates does is staged and calculated.

"Mexican nationals near Falfurrias, going north on horseback?" Moates taps the map with the pool cue. "This position makes no sense unless they are trying to avoid being seen."

"How many are there?" Miller asks.

Moates shrugs. "You've read the telegram. It doesn't say."

"This is too vague," Miller repeats, looking back down at the paper. "The direction they're heading is ambiguous, at best."

"The direction they're heading is *north*, toward San Diego. I shouldn't have to remind you what that might imply. Can you think of any good reason why a contingent of Mexicans would be moving on horseback, with pack animals, through that God-forsaken country?"

"Well, yes sir, I can," Miller says. "Any number of perfectly legitimate reasons. Vaqueros looking for work. Or going home from somewhere else. Good Lord, they could be *anybody*."

"Sergeant, we are not here to debate this." Moates' anger is palpable. "South Texas is a powder-keg. Laredo itself is eighty percent Mexican, and the revolution starts halfway across that bridge over there." Moates points vaguely to the west, with a dismissive gesture. "These bastards want to take everything we've worked so hard for. Parasites."

"What are you proposing we do?" Miller asks.

Moates leans back in his chair and regards Miller with an odd, detached intensity. "I am not *proposing* anything. I am *telling* you what we are going to do. You and your men will all be taking the 5:15 tomorrow morning to Corpus Christi. Parsons will have an extra stock car coupled on for our use." He rises to his feet and turns again to the map and points to the hatched line designating the Texas-Mexican Railroad. "Leave Hardesty for coverage here. You and Asher and Teeter will meet Burnett and Anspach at Hebbronville."

"And then we do . . . what?" Miller is genuinely perplexed.

"Head due east to cover Duval County south of the rail line." Moates taps the map. "Go as far as the Jim Wells County line and then head back. You should intersect either these men or their tracks."

"And if we do?"

"Assess the situation. If you don't find anything, head to San Diego on Friday afternoon and return here."

Miller pulls a watch from his vest pocket and regards it. "It is 11:30," he says. "The animals we can get ready. What about supplies?"

Moates is prepared. "Jackman will open up for an hour at 4:00. Put everything on account. You'll need food and tack for three or four days. Make you have any necessary ordnance. Have the horses and gear and pack mules and all supplies ready on the siding by 4:45. Remember to take horses for Burnett and Anspach. All they need to do is be in Hebbronville at 9:00 tomorrow morning. I don't want them to have *any* excuse not to be there. I will want to address the three of you before you pull out." Moates stands up. "That's all."

"That's *not* all, sir," Miller says, as genially as he can. "I'd rather take Hardesty and leave Asher."

"No." Moates shakes his head emphatically.

"I don't understand your dislike of Asher."

"I don't dislike him. He's just dead weight. It is time for him to either fish or cut bait."

Miller is silent for a moment, and Moates interprets this as a thoughtful reflection of the order. It is no such thing. Miller is angry, and he is holding himself in reserve until his emotions subside. He nods and tries another approach: "Hardesty would be better able to help us with this particular job."

"That would be true no matter what the job was. I know that Asher is ailing, and I know that he has been a Ranger for a long time."

Moates walks around the desk, and Miller reflexively rises from his chair. "But enough is enough. If this exercise is too strenuous for him, and it will be, I will have the justification I need to send him on his way. Really, Horace, it's in everyone's best interest, including his. The Rangers budget and roster is the lowest it has ever been. We need good, productive, dependable men. Asher is long past his prime."

Miller finally surrenders on this issue and raises a second point of concern. "I would prefer not to use Burnett," he says. "We have enough men without him."

"No," Moates says again, and now Miller can see that this request visibly irritates Moates, where the first one did not.

"Teeter is brand-spanking new," Miller says, just for the record. Teeter has just been sworn in less than two weeks ago and is untested.

"Let's see what he's made of," Moates says.

And that is all. Miller returns home in the midnight cold to find Leona, his wife, waiting for him, sitting at the dining table. She goes into the kitchen and returns with two cups of coffee.

"How long?" she asks.

"Three or four days. Complete and utter waste of time and resources. I don't see why we can't just have Burnett or Anspach do this."

Miller telephones Anspach in Alice and asks him to get word to Burnett, who is already in Hebbronville, that they both need to be at the depot in Hebbronville at 9:00 the next morning. He then contacts Hardesty and informs him that he is being held in reserve to see that Webb County is competently covered while the rest of its Laredo Rangers are away. Hardesty takes it stoically, and Miller asks him to have Asher and Teeter at Jackman's Supply Store by 4:00.

By 3:00, Hardesty is able to get Teeter on the telephone, but because Asher has no telephone, he sends Teeter over to rouse him from his room at the Sirocco Hotel.

So, at 3:25 on Wednesday morning, Teeter crosses Jarvis Plaza to the hotel and enters through the large front doors to the long oak counter, where a portly old man reads a newspaper.

"Asher's room," Teeter says.

The clerk motions to a wide staircase on the right. "Top floor. 617."

Teeter sees no elevator, so he moves to the stairs and begins the climb with a young man's energy. The second and third floors are beautifully carpeted and well-lit; these are the guest floors. Four and five are darker, and the carpeting is much more worn, and Teeter realizes that these are the residence floors. At six, the carpeting is all but gone, and there is a single dim bulb in the hallway. Teeter realizes from the sheet-covered furniture lining one wall of the corridor that this floor is used mostly for storage. Half of the rooms have no numbers, but at the end of the hallway, he finds Asher's room and knocks gently.

From inside, he hears the faint sound of moving bedsprings, a momentary silence, and then the striking of a match. A soft light begins to glow beneath the door. The bedsprings quietly churn again, giving up some small weight, and quick, light footsteps approach the door, which then begins to open to the inside until stopped by the length of the latch chain.

A woman's face, lit dimly by the lamp held in her raised left hand, fills the gap between the door and the frame, and Teeter recognizes her at once, even in the half-light. With his surprise, a memory surfaces, warm and pleasant, and an image comes to his mind, unbidden but welcome, and emotionally sensual. He remembers her brushing her long, graying hair as they exchanged pre-embrace pleasantries.

Teeter sees no recognition in her face. "Yes?" she says.

"I have a message for Mister Asher. From Sergeant Miller. We're being called into the field. He needs us at Jackman's to get supplies in thirty minutes, and then to the livery stable, and then to the depot. Train, then horseback. Three or four days, Miller says."

As the woman quietly digests this, Teeter says, "We've met before."

"No," the woman says, too quickly. She seems startled.

"Yes. Odessa. Couple years ago."

"No," she says again and steps back. "Thank you." The door closes, and Teeter is alone again in the dark hallway. He goes back downstairs; he needs to reassure Hardesty that Asher has been informed.

Inside the room, Beulah Asher steps over to the large table by the bay window overlooking the plaza, puts down the lamp, and leans on the table's edge, elbows locked and head down, trying to regain her composure. She has been dreading this moment for a long while, and the suddenness of its arrival has left her drained. She could easily surrender to a flood of tears, but there is no time and no point.

She moves across the room to the bed and looks down at her husband. She does not want to rouse him. His sleep is narcotic-deep, head thrown back, raspy-rattle breathing with a thick, pinkish drool covering the pillow beneath his open mouth. Her gaze moves to the laudanum bottle on the table beside the bed, and she sees that he has had to take some during the night to sleep. She has begun to worry that he has started taking more than the pain really requires.

Beulah readies herself and then reaches out and touches his shoulder, gently at first, and then more firmly when there is no response.

"Thomas," she says. "Thomas, you need to wake up."

His unfocused eyes open and finally settle on hers as he climbs up from his sulfurous dreams. Beulah sees understanding come over his face, and he slowly works his way into a sitting position on the side of the bed, with her arm around his shoulders for support. His own hands are down deep between his knees. He is trembling in the cold room.

"What time is it?" he asks.

"Half-past three. Man was just here. Says Miller sent him. You're being called up. Mounted. Three or four days."

"What man?" Asher is slowly digesting this.

"Young. Just a kid. Maybe twenty-five."

"Teeter," Asher says. "He's new." He gets warily to his feet and reaches for his pants, draped over the end of the bed. But his bladder kicks in, and he moves unsteadily to the door and down the hallway to the bathroom. As he urinates, the pain begins in his lower back, concurrent with that undefinable need for some laudanum. His awakening mind begins to sense the implications. He finishes and moves back down the corridor to his room and sits down at the table. Beulah is still sitting on his side of the bed, facing the far wall, her hands in her lap.

"I don't know what to do," he says.

Beulah sits for a moment and then she stands and picks up the laudanum bottle from the side of the bed and walks over to the table. She puts it on top of the battered Bible that Asher reads from during his prayer time, next to the copy of *Middlemarch* that she reveres enough to begin rereading every time she finishes it. She sits down across the table from him. Asher takes a sip of the laudanum and waits for the familiar glow to begin to take hold.

"There is no way you can sit a horse for three days," Beulah says.

Asher holds up the bottle of laudanum.

"That doesn't help a thing," Beulah says sharply. "It won't even *begin* to get you through this."

Asher shrugs. "I got nothing to lose by trying."

Beulah is quiet at this, and now Asher realizes that something else is happening here. "What's wrong?"

"He recognized me," Beulah says flatly. "From Odessa."

"Teeter?" Asher considers this. "Do you remember *him*?"

Beulah is silent. If she says *yes*, it means that Teeter was memorable. If she says *no*, it will remind Asher that there were so many men. Either answer will hurt Asher, and this is a notion that distresses her.

Asher tries to remember if this is how he imagined he would feel when this moment came, and he is surprised to find that he is vexed and embarrassed. He is not angry with Beulah; he had promised himself repeatedly that he would not be. He had it in his mind that he was going to be the model of patient, forgiving rectitude. But now that the moment has actually arrived, he finds himself ill-equipped to know what to do or say, to Beulah or anyone else.

He changes the subject. "Where do I go, and when?"

"Jackman's at four for supplies, depot at five with the horses."

"Did he say what it's about?"

"No."

Asher sits thinking, and there is no good option. "How much we got saved?" he asks.

"Two-hundred and seventy dollars."

"Two-hundred and seventy dollars," Asher says. "If I do go, it will hurt, but maybe I can do it and stay on the payroll."

"I can't believe that Miller is asking you to do this," Beulah says. "He knows how much you are hurting."

"It ain't Miller asking. It's Moates telling." Asher stands and moves to the bed and begins to put on his clothes, wincing all the while. "Hell with him. I can do this." This is false bravado, and Asher knows it, and he knows that Beulah knows it. He dresses and packs a change of clothes, and his laudanum, as well as the new, unopened reserve bottle, which he wraps carefully in a red rag. As he leaves, he hesitates at the door and turns to Beulah.

"This don't matter," Asher says.

2

J ust after five o'clock, after the supplies from Jackman's and the horses
and pack mules and tack have been loaded onto the stock car, the
four Rangers stand on the depot platform in the pre-dawn cold. Miller
has not given Teeter or Asher much detail about what they are doing
there because he does not want to irritate Moates by robbing him of the
pleasure of telling the men himself of the task ahead of them.

Moates is speaking now, and the men listen with polite attention,
and Asher is starting to sense the way of things; Teeter is simply too
new. There are too few specifics, and too many exhortations concerning
"vigilance" and "professionalism." Miller, standing behind Moates, can
see a cynical resignation come slowly to Asher's face, and he is dismayed
with Moates' willingness to let ambition cloud his judgment.

"So that's it," Moates concludes. "You will be briefed in the field
concerning your specific objectives." He steps to one side. "I have asked

the Reverend Jacobs to dedicate this effort in prayer." Standing just behind Moates, the Very Reverend Roscoe Jacobs of the Second Presbyterian Church of Laredo, Texas begins to speak.

"Oh, Lord, we do ask you to give these men safe passage to their destination and a quick resolution to their task. Bind them in righteousness and let their light shine in this dark world. We humbly implore these things. Amen."

The men start to move away, and Miller steps forward. "Can I get one of you to stay with the horses in the stock car?"

"I'll do it," Asher says. He is already anticipating the need for concealed access to his laudanum.

"Me, too," Teeter says, and now Asher knows how the next several hours are going to unfold.

Asher and Teeter cross into the stock car and find that the horses and pack mules have already been tethered into their rough stalls. They are eating hay, which has been laid in front of each of them. The pack mules have not been loaded down yet; the supplies sit on one end of the car. The air is pungent with the smell of horse droppings.

Asher stands by the sliding door of the car and looks out to the platform at Miller, who has walked up and taken the heavy metal handle of the door in his hand. "See you in Hebbronville," Miller says. "About four hours." Asher nods, and Miller slides the door shut.

There is an oil lantern suspended from the ceiling of the car, and as the train slowly starts to move forward, shadows begin to dance on the sides of the dim interior, frantically at first, but as the train settles into its rhythm, they become more languid. Asher walks over to a line of saddles against the wall and picks up his own, which he carries over to the closed loading door and drops. Sitting down gingerly upon it, he leans back, eyes Teeter, and waits.

The miles pass and Asher begins to wonder if Teeter is having difficulty summoning the courage to start the conversation. Teeter is sitting on the floor of the opposite wall, legs stretched out in front of him, his hat in his hands.

Finally, Teeter says, "What do you think about all this?"

"Not much."

"I think it's exciting."

A renewed silence ensues now for a while. The train has ramped up to full speed, and the union of movement and sound has resolved itself into a gentle emotional cushion. Asher thinks of Beulah, back in their room, and he wishes that he had left her with a more reassuring demeanor. He imagines the things he might better have said to her to relieve her anxieties.

The pain begins again, low in Asher's back, and he knows now just how much riding the sorrel is going to hurt. He should have known better than to decide, while the laudanum was working its magic, that he could handle it. He wants very badly to pull the half-consumed bottle from the inside pocket of his coat, unroll it from the protective rag wrapped around it, and take a few sips, but Teeter is regarding him quietly. Asher can see that he is trying to figure out how to initiate the conversation that they both know is coming.

The miles pass quietly for a time, and then Teeter says, as casually as he knows how, "So, how long you folks been married?"

"*There* it is," Asher says, and smiles.

"Say what?"

"Been wondering how you were going to get into it."

Teeter regards him for a moment. He now realizes that elliptical conversation is going to be pointless. "I met her once," he says. "Probably before you did."

Asher is struck suddenly by the thought that he does not know why Teeter wants to discuss this with him at all. He had hoped that having recognized Beulah, Teeter would just let the matter drop. After all, if Teeter wants to share his knowledge of Beulah's past, it will not reflect well on himself. He can think of only two reasons why Teeter is pursuing this: he wants to know if Asher knows, and he wants Asher to know that *he* knows.

"Teeter, there just ain't any advantage you have in this. None. What's past is past. I hope you do the right thing, and just keep this to yourself." Asher says this gently, smiling, trying to convey kinship.

"It don't bother you that I been with her? Along with all them other men?"

For an instant, anger wells up in Asher so strongly that he wonders if he can control it. He wants to move across the car and throttle this cur to regret. But the anger is tempered with caution, and he checks it immediately. He knows that this act would guarantee knowledge of Beulah's past to everyone, and he does not know if Teeter can or will be discreet. It will be another four days before he becomes aware that Teeter has already been indiscreet.

"Of course, it bothers me," Asher says, "but not like you think. I didn't meet her the way you did, and I don't think of her the way you do. I get a picture in my mind of you with her and, hell yes, it hurts. But she was in a bad place in her life then. If you feel obliged to pass this on, you will be hurting her considerable, and me, and for nothing."

Teeter exhales now, with the relief of a man holding four aces. He feels now that *he* is driving the conversation, and that he can get all the knowledge he wants, and that Asher is powerless to object.

"Tell me how you met," Teeter says.

"That ain't none of your business," Asher replies, without hesitation. He rises painfully to his feet and crosses the width of the car and looks down at the startled young man. "You are going to do what you are going to do. I am asking you for mercy. She's building a new life here, with me. You mouth off, we got to pick up and leave. That's all this means. I am asking you to leave us be. That way, we can maybe stay here, and you don't have to have people picturing *you* in a whorehouse."

Teeter is nodding now, emphatically. "Sure. Hey, I was just curious, that's all. Didn't mean nothing by it." He rises nervously to his feet and extends his hand, which Asher takes. "Between us," Teeter says. "Never happened." Teeter wishes now that he had not told Hardesty.

Things are quiet for the next several hours. Teeter sits back down, and leans back against the wall, and closes his eyes, and Asher retreats to the rear of the car and stands next to the sorrel. He is vexed to the point of not being able to shrug it off. He hurts, and he leans forward, his head on a flank of the horse. He is tired, and he wishes that he had begged off this trip, to let things develop however they would have on their own. The laudanum is in his hands now, and he takes a sip and waits for the pain to fade away.

The relief comes, but the anger remains.

An hour after dawn, the locomotive expels a loud whistle, and begins to slow down; it is time for Miller's team to exit the train, which comes gradually to a stop. There is a long pause, then the sliding door to the freight car is opened from the outside, and Miller, Burnett, and Anspach are standing, not at the Hebbronville depot, but on hard ground just beyond it. They pull the gangplank out from beneath the car and latch it into place. One-by-one, Asher leads each mount to the door, along with the corresponding tack, and the Ranger who will use it walks up to the top of the gangplank to take the animal's halter. During this process, Teeter is loading the two pack mules with their supplies. Finally, Miller's team is standing beside the train as it pulls away.

When it has moved down the tracks far enough to allow conversation, Miller pulls a map from the inside of his coat, drops to one knee, and spreads it out on the ground. The men form a circle around it.

With the addition of the two new men, Miller's team is now complete. Anspach is an earnest young man who has come to South Texas from New Mexico. He is not much older than Teeter. He is a good Ranger, and his fluent Spanish makes him invaluable.

Burnett is older, and irritatingly gregarious, especially when he has been drinking. Miller trusts Burnett the least of these men, but Burnett served with Render Moates in Cuba, and Moates protects him.

"The way I see it," Miller says, breath frosting, "we need to head due east. They could be anywhere along this line." He motions on the map with a gloved index finger. "With any luck, we intercept either the riders or their trail sometime in the next twenty-four hours."

No one says anything, and Miller puts the map away and stands. They all mount their horses, and Teeter and Asher each take the reins of a pack mule.

Asher has prepared for this moment with a liberal dose of laudanum, and he is able to pull himself up into the saddle without too much pain. But when he sits back, the pain becomes so acute so quickly that he instinctively finds himself standing in the stirrups. They begin to move east at a brisk pace, away from the town, and now begins, for Asher, the exquisite agony of riding horseback. He stays high in the saddle, his backside making little contact, until his legs become so tired that he has to take the weight off them. Then the pain from his lower back, exacerbated by the up and down motion of the hard saddle, becomes rapidly so intolerable that he stands again. Each cycle becomes shorter until he is finally forced to pull gently back on the sorrel's reins and allow the others to move ahead of him. This affords him the privacy necessary to pull the laudanum bottle from his coat and take a large sip. After a few moments the pain fades to something manageable, but Asher knows that this will be short-lived. He also knows that he will go through his laudanum too quickly if he doesn't ration it somehow. A slow, simmering despair begins to set in.

At mid-morning, they are still on relatively flat ground, traversing mile after mile of scrubland that the map says will yield gradually to a slight rise, and then a rockier, uneven terrain. Miller knows that technically they are on private land: either one of the large ranches, or one of the massive, corporately owned holdings of the petroleum companies. He knows that to their east lies the King Ranch, majestic in size and wealth, and to the north is the Diamond-D, and then the Ladder, and beyond even that the Maragon-McKay. To their south lies the vast Red River DM.

Early in the afternoon, Miller brings them to a stop with a raised hand. The day has warmed some, but the scrubland air is still brisk. There is not a cloud in the sky.

"We need to rest the horses a spell," Miller says, and they all climb down and awkwardly stretch their legs and empty their bladders.

"How accessible is the jerky?" Miller asks.

"I packed it right near the top," Teeter says, and he moves over to one of the pack mules and unties a cloth bag from the top of the bundle. He puts it on the ground and removes some cured meat from the pouch and passes it over to the others. One-by-one, they each draw their knives and cut a wedge, and stand there, alternately chewing the jerky and taking swigs from their canteens. Except for Asher, who leans into his horse, with his head against the side of the saddle.

"You okay?" Miller asks him.

Asher nods, without looking at him. "Just stiff." All Asher wants is to get back on the trail, so that he can lag behind with his opiate.

Miller pulls out his map again, and the men again look down at it on the ground. Miller taps a spot several inches east of Hebbronville and says, "I make us out to be *here*. We're making good time, but we still need to pick it up a bit." He points farther to the right, along some imaginary line, and taps a second spot. "If we can make it *here* by dark, we will be in a good position to begin the day tomorrow." He refolds the map and stands back up, and they all mount their horses and begin heading southeast.

Asher, still in serious discomfort, allows himself to fall to the back of the pack, and again he goes to the laudanum for relief. He has a full bottle packed away in his saddlebag, but he is growing concerned about how quickly the partial bottle is disappearing. His troubled mind is now calculating the exact relationship between time, distance, and the volume of the laudanum. He concludes that if he can keep the full bottle available for the morrow, he will have enough to ride somewhere to get more. He knows that he will have to talk to Miller and explain things and that his time as a Texas Ranger, so important to him for reasons that he cannot fully articulate to Beulah, will have to come to an end. He hurts too much to care any longer.

But Miller has been watching Asher closely, and he is growing concerned. Miller knows of Asher's back and has asked him several times about it, only to be reassured that it won't interfere with his job. Now he has noticed Asher's lagging to the rear, and he suspects that

Asher is using the privacy to get relief somehow. Miller is a kind man at heart, and he does not like seeing Asher in pain, but he has a job to do. After pondering this for a while, Miller slows his horse down a bit and waits for the other riders to pass. Then he falls in beside Asher.

"How bad is it?"

Asher looks over at him, grimacing, and he doesn't even try to evade the question. "I don't think I can go too much farther," he says. "We make camp tonight. In the morning, I'll just go on to Falfurrias." He stands up in the stirrups for a moment and then settles back down again, and Miller can see the pain on his face. "I know it's over," Asher says. "Sorry, Miller. I should've known better."

"It doesn't matter," Miller says. "If you can make it to camp, we'll see how it goes from there." Asher nods, and Miller spurs his horse back up to take the lead.

They continue at a good pace through the afternoon hours, and the light begins to change as the day draws to a close. Right at sunset, when Miller expects about thirty minutes of visibility left, he pulls up and announces, "We'll put down here for the night." Wearily the men dismount and begin the process of setting up a hasty camp. The horses are unsaddled, the supplies are removed from the pack mules, and a fire is made. Teeter, being the youngest and newest of them, is the assigned cook, and he begins the preparations to make some hot stew and coffee. The men set their bedrolls out around the fire, in no particular order. Without a word of explanation, Asher puts himself down a bit farther away from them.

After dinner, Miller asks the men to coordinate a watch schedule. Asher announces, with no room for discussion, that he will go first.

Each Ranger on watch does a consistent job of keeping wood on the fire, so the cold of the night, which hovers about ten degrees above freezing, does not thoroughly penetrate the bones of the men as they sleep. At dawn, they are up to a hot breakfast of coffee and flapjacks, which Teeter has dutifully prepared for them during the preceding hour.

Asher has had a painful night, but he has been able to sleep fitfully, awakening every hour or so for a pull on the laudanum. He is surprised to begin the morning with half an inch of the amber fluid still at the bottom of the first bottle. As he is saddling the sorrel, Miller walks up to him and says, with obvious concern, "What do you intend to do?"

"Sergeant, I'm done for. I am worthless to you. I will go with you to the county line, head east to Falfurrias, and catch a train back to Laredo. I resign, effective immediately." He looks over at Miller, who is standing with no expression but pursed lips. "Sorry to let you down. This should get Moates off your back."

Miller nods slowly and shrugs. "I'm sorry, too. You've been a good Ranger, and you got hurt in the line of duty. I wish there was something I could do."

"I wish there was, too," Asher says. "But there ain't."

Miller walks back over to the campfire, which the men are extinguishing with kicked dirt. He pulls the map out again and bends down. "We are here," he says, pointing. "We should be able to head due east. If they are there, we will find them."

"What if they haven't got this far north yet?" Anspach asks. "We'd be way too far east before they come up."

Miller has an answer for this. "We got to get just here," and he points again to the Duval–Jim Wells County line. "Any farther east from that point is beyond our ability to intercept them. We get there, and we just turn around and head back in this direction. If we continue going back and forth for the next day or two, we should find them, if they are coming up this far west."

"We could split up," Burnett says. "String it out, and then regroup when one of us sees something."

There is something in Burnett's voice that catches Miller off guard. The words are a bit slurred, and spoken with an unnatural cadence. Miller glances up at him, and he sees that Burnett's eyes are a little unfocused. A realization immediately comes to him.

"Have you been drinking?" Miller asks.

"No," Burnett says. He stares at Miller intently, who stares back at him, and then he turns his head up to the other men and shrugs and smiles, and says, "Well, maybe a little."

"Damn it," Miller says. "Where's the bottle?"

"Drunk it," Burnett says. "Every damn drop of it. It got cold last night." He smiles again.

"Was that all of it?" Miller is furious.

"Yup."

"You stay by me," Miller says. "Do you understand me? Until you sober up, you don't leave my sight."

"You're in charge," Burnett says. He smiles yet again.

Thirty minutes later they are moving steadily into the sunrise, with Anspach on point, keeping an eye on the landscape both around them and under them, looking for either riders or tracks. Asher figures that it is only another ten miles or so before he cuts out to Falfurrias, so he loosens up a little with the remaining laudanum. The pain is subdued.

They don't get ten miles. Less than four miles from camp, Anspach pulls up suddenly and reaches into his saddlebag for his field glasses. He gazes through them at a spot on the distant horizon.

The others have stopped now, and Miller says, "What is it?" He can see nothing on the horizon at all.

"Saw *something*," Anspach says, "I *know* I did." He is moving the glasses now, ever so slightly, back and forth. He stops and says, "There. Just . . . *there*." He points, and passes the glasses over to Miller, who raises them, scans the horizon, and settles in on the distant figure.

"One rider," Miller says. "One pack mule." He passes the glasses back to Anspach. "He looks harmless. We ride at him single file. We just want to talk to him. We don't want to scare him. Am I understood?"

"It could be a trap," Burnett says.

"Shut up," Miller says. He will wonder later if the harshness of his tone might have affected what will come next.

He leads the men forward again, taking point himself. In ten minutes, they come up to the figure on horseback.

It is an old man, clearly Mexican, with a tired, lined face, and an anxious smile that, oddly, does not seem forced. He comes to a stop as the Rangers move around him, and he regards them nervously.

"*Buenos Dias señores,*" the old man says.

"*Buenos Dias señor,*" Miller replies. "Do you speak English?"

The old man smiles and shakes his head. "*No señor, lo siento.*"

Miller looks to Anspach for help with the conversation. "Tell him not to be frightened, but that we have some questions for him."

Anspach speaks to the old man, who visibly relaxes.

"Tell him we are looking for a group of mounted men, from Mexico, heading in the same direction he is. Ask him if he has seen them, or ridden with them."

Anspach relays this to the old man, who shakes his head.

"This greaser is lying," Burnett says. "I can smell it."

"Burnett," Miller says, "I said shut up, and I meant it."

"Suit yourself," Burnett says.

The harshness of the words between the two men startles the Mexican, who looks suddenly apprehensive.

"*Cuál es el problema?*" he asks Anspach.

"Tell him not to worry," Miller says, looking away from Burnett.

"*Nada,*" Anspach says to the old man.

"Ask him his name, please," Miller says.

"*Cuál es tu nombre?*" Anspach asks.

"*Sanchez,*" replies the old man, relaxed again, bowing his head formally and touching the front tip of his sombrero. "*Emilio Sanchez.*"

"Ask Mr. Sanchez where he is going, and why."

Anspach translates the question, and the old man smiles again and starts to speak rapidly, pointing back over his shoulder to the south, and then pointing north. When he finishes, Anspach asks him a further question, resulting in another animated, voluble response. Anspach turns to Miller.

"Sir, this man don't seem quite right in the head. He seems excited about something, like a little kid with a secret. He says he's on his way to San Diego to get something special to take back to Mexico."

"San Diego," Miller says. "Did you ask him what it is he is getting?"

"He doesn't say what," Anspach says.

"We need to know what it is," Miller says, and Anspach passes the question over.

The old man smiles again and then raises his forefinger in the air as though something has just occurred to him. He reaches under his weathered serape as he says, "*Aqui. Deja que te enseñe.*"

And then everything goes very wrong.

"Son of a bitch has a gun," Burnett shouts, and his hand comes away from his holster, and he is pointing his Colt, and the hammer has been pulled back. Two things happen simultaneously: Burnett yells something guttural, and the weapon discharges and bucks in his hand.

All of the horses jump in the crisp morning air.

The old man, still smiling, looks down to his stomach.

"Good Lord Almighty," Asher says.

C onsider the immediate effect of the sudden, unintended violence on the six men sitting on their six startled, skittish horses. Imagine the sound of the explosion in the cold, sharp morning air, and the voluminous smoke that mists instantly around them, and the odor of cordite that will linger on their clothes until they are next laundered. These are all sense impressions that they will remember in retrospect, but which have come into being so quickly that their minds cannot immediately grasp what has just happened. In many ways, the disorientation that they feel will linger for the rest of their lives, which will range in duration from twelve hours to sixty-one years.

Let us look first at Cord Burnett, who will later regard his behavior with a feeling of disconnection, as though he is remembering the actions and reactions of someone else. His Colt has just discharged, to his complete astonishment, and his arm has recoiled into the air, and his gun hand tingles from the blast. His horse steps backward with enough energy to cause him to lose his balance in the saddle, and he instinctively grabs the horn with his other hand and squeezes his inner thighs against the animal and steadies himself. For some reason, unknown even to himself, he laughs out loud. His mind clears, and his gaze moves involuntarily to Miller. But Miller is regarding the Mexican with a face that is moving from surprise to depthless regret. Burnett now looks over to Sanchez, and he knows in that instant that his life has just come undone.

Let us regard Horace Miller, who is the first of them to realize what has just happened, and who is the only one of them temporarily deafened by the sound of the discharge. There is an uncomfortable ringing in his ears, and he unconsciously strains to hear something, *anything*, that will bring all of his senses back to him. He is already beginning to consider ways to explain it all away, to his later shame when he will think back on it. He knows that the other men will be looking to him for direction in short order, and he is considering which expression he wants his face to display. Such are the instincts of leadership.

Let us examine Gerald Anspach, who has been interrupted in mid-conversation so suddenly that he is still translating in his mind the Mexican's last utterance, even as he struggles to settle down his horse. "*Aqui,*" the old man had said. "Here." Then . . . what? "*Deja que te enseñe.*" Ludicrously, Anspach formulates, "Let me show you." And now the picture is complete in his mind. The Mexican was reaching for something under his serape, in his shirt perhaps, when Burnett shot him. Had Burnett seen something in the man's gesture that he had not?

Let us spend a moment with Lyle Teeter, who is a simple young man and who will have the easiest time dealing with what has just happened. There will be no introspection about this with Teeter, other than an attempt later to gain some advantage from it. There is just the momentary surprise, then the slow understanding, and then the great shrug, which portends the way he will live his long, empty, colorless life.

Let us observe Thomas Asher. It is Asher who has spoken first, being the most overtly religious of the Rangers, but his words were not really of a spiritual bent. Rather, they were a cultural expression of surprise, although this is a distinction that would be regarded with indifference by every man there. Asher's immediate thoughts are different from the others because Asher's situation is different: how will this affect his access to his laudanum? He holds any sense of panic in check because he instinctively realizes that this could go either way: this could all just as easily *accelerate* his relief as extend his pain. These are transient thoughts in his mind, largely unformed, but they are there, they are his first, and they will later be the source of some measure of guilt and regret.

Let us finally consider Emilio Sanchez, who struggles for comprehension. He had been reaching for the paper in his shirt pocket when, for some incomprehensible reason, the gringo with the glassy eyes raised a pistol and shot him. He felt the bullet graze his wrist, and then he felt an almost simultaneous punch to his stomach, and then he lost his breath, for just an instant. But he breathes in again now, almost immediately. He is having trouble understanding what has just happened. He cannot find linkage in his mind between reaching for the telegram, in a spirit of cooperation, and what followed. He is surprised that the force of the bullet has not knocked him backward out of his saddle. He looks down at his stomach, hoping against hope that the bullet has struck something which has, in turn, struck him, a coin perhaps, but he sees the hole in the serape, and he reaches down to move it out of the way, to see what is beneath it. His wrist is beginning to hurt now, the first of the pain that will surely follow, radiating a vibrating discomfort up to his elbow, and now he sees the hole in his shirt and feels the thick, warm liquid begin to flow down the front of him. As he considers this, he feels that same warmth begin to flow into the crease of his buttocks, and he realizes that the bullet must have gone completely through him.

He glances back up now, and his gaze moves instinctively to Miller, and Sanchez can see in Miller's face a confirmation of what he has just this moment started to realize. The old man's smile fades, and what is left is a look of profound sadness that will long haunt the memories of every Ranger there, except for Teeter.

He has not pictured a death such as this. He has always imagined it as a serene thing: lying in the dim interior of his adobe hovel, with the priest performing extreme unction by candlelight, or the sudden darkness as his old heart just stops, or simply not waking from sleep. He wonders if this is a judgment from God for his wayward life: for all the tequila, and for all the indolence, and, in his younger days, for all the whores he would frequent when he could get a few pesos together. He has confessed these things to the priest back in Matamoros, so he is not so afraid of hell. He is merely trying to make sense of this.

His gaze shifts now to Burnett, who is regarding him with a ludicrous and unthinking expression that remains from his laughter. He had laughed, it occurs to Sanchez. He had *laughed.* "*Por qué has hecho esto?*" he asks, as he shakes his head in utter wonder.

"He wants to know why you have done this," Anspach says, looking at Burnett. "So do the rest of us, I think."

Burnett responds immediately. "I thought he was reaching for a gun." But then his foggy mind instantly realizes that this explanation makes it sound like he *intended* for the Colt to discharge, which is not true. "It was an accident," he says, and then his shame silences him.

Anspach looks at the Mexican and starts to translate, but then it occurs to him that the old man's question was rhetorical.

Sanchez, to the sudden surprise of everyone, is now slowly climbing down from his horse. He is doing it in the fluid way that any man would dismount, his right leg coming back and over the horse's rear, and then planting itself on the hard ground. He removes his left foot from the stirrup and bends over, placing both hands on his knees. It becomes obvious that he cannot quite seem to get his breath.

Anspach dismounts and walks over to him and places one hand on his shoulder. He does this because he feels somehow the closest to the old man because he had been the one engaged in direct conversation with him. He worries vaguely that this gesture is going to commit him to something he would rather avoid, but he would rather risk that than seem indifferent to the old man about what is happening.

Sanchez looks up at Anspach from his stooped position and his expression is one of accepting sorrow. "*Que Dios tenga misericordia de mi alma,*" he says softly. Tears come to Anspach's eyes, and he looks away.

"What did he just say?" Miller asks.

"May God have mercy on my soul," Anspach says, and for a moment Miller is perplexed. Then he realizes that Anspach is giving him a direct translation, and not a personal *mea culpa*.

Miller sits in his saddle, thinking.

The men are still mounted, except for Anspach. The Mexican has decided to stop standing and, with Anspach's help, has dropped to one knee, and now sags awkwardly into a sitting position right where he had been standing. There are so many things happening all at once that Miller feels numbed with indecision. How can he determine the best course of action when he can't seem to get fixed in his mind what options there are, much less understand what has just happened?

"Dismount," he says, and the men climb down from their horses. Now they all simply stand stiffly, holding their reins. None of them, except Anspach, can bear to look at the old man.

The first thing to do is to try to assess the Mexican's injury. Miller drops his reins and walks over to Sanchez and squats down beside him. Sanchez looks at him, and it occurs now to Miller that the old man is waiting for direction from him every bit as much as are his men, and this realization somehow makes him feel an immediate inadequacy.

Miller lifts the serape, and he immediately knows that it is hopeless. An image comes to his mind, long repressed: Corporal Anderson, sitting on the south slope of Moro Crater, in the Philippines. That was nine years ago, but Miller remembers it vividly. Anderson's wound did not seem as bad as this one, but he died quickly and in great anguish. Miller had been the officer standing nearest to him, so Anderson had been staring at him intently, begging for relief, while he and his men just stood there, looking down at him. Miller had been about to say something to him when he saw the light go right out of his eyes, and suddenly the corporal was looking *through* Miller, rather than *at* him.

"Do you think he can ride?" Anspach asks.

Miller stands up and regards his men. He doesn't want to say a single thing that the Mexican might comprehend, but that doesn't matter, not really, because he doesn't feel like talking to any of them anyway. Anspach and Teeter are too green to offer meaningful advice, Asher is wrestling with his own demons, and Burnett he wants to beat senseless. He has never felt such a sense of burden in his life.

He glances around him at the terrain and sees no landmark of any sort. It is still flat scrub-country, with sparse vegetation, not useful for much, except perhaps for the minerals or oil beneath it. He pulls his map from his coat pocket, crouches back down, and spreads it on the ground. This time, no one walks up to stand over it.

He cannot be sure, but he believes that they must be very close to the southern border of Duval County, about half-way between Hebbronville and Falfurrias. It is relatively desolate here, perhaps fifteen or twenty miles to the nearest town of any sort. The map he uses is not granular enough to show homesteads, and they could wander for hours looking for one, and still find nothing. Five miles or so to the south, the Arroyo Baluarte snakes eastward through the western part of the newly established Jim Hogg County and the majority of northern Brooks County.

He leaves the map spread out on the ground and stands up again. His mind is now functioning analytically, and he performs his inner calculations, and his conclusion is bleak and discouraging.

"This man is gut-shot," he says finally, matter-of-factly, "and I don't know what we can do for him. We are maybe a day's ride from any help, and he will probably live for just another couple of hours. In a little while, the shock is going to wear off, and he will be in horrible pain. I can't see trying to put him on a horse. I just can't see it. It would be terrible for him." His voice trails off, not because he doesn't know what to say next, but because he doesn't want to say it.

"What should we do?" Anspach asks, from behind him. Miller turns around and sees Anspach regarding him with an expression of genuine deference. Sanchez is now lying down, on his left side, facing away, with his hands out of sight in front of him. Miller is relieved that the Mexican does not seem to be following the conversation at all.

"I am only weighing our options," Miller says. "I am open to any suggestion at all."

"There's only one thing we can do," Burnett starts to say.

But Miller stops him cold. "Shut up," he says one final time, almost shouting. "Burnett, look what you have done. Just *look* at it." Miller suddenly thinks of a productive way to vent his anger, and he walks over to Burnett and says, "I need your sidearm."

Without hesitating, Burnett pulls his Colt back out of his holster and hands it, butt-first, to Miller. He speaks no more that day.

Miller turns back to the others. "There is nothing we can do here for this poor man," he says. "Nothing. I wish there was, but there isn't."

"We could show him the respect of staying here with him until it is over," Anspach says.

"I'm sorry, but I don't see it," Miller says. "We need to continue the search through tomorrow, and then head north to be in San Diego by late afternoon. It won't make the slightest difference to him. I know that's cold, but there it is."

There is another silence, this time protracted, as five men search their hearts, and find them wanting.

After a moment, Miller says, looking at Anspach, "So here we are: I need a volunteer to stay with him."

Anspach now regrets climbing down to help the Mexican. He hasn't done him any good, not really, and now Miller is clearly suggesting that he remove himself from the action. He is thinking that he should have thought it through and resisted his natural inclination.

Burnett is now beginning to sober up, and that, coupled with his complete and total embarrassment and humiliation, is all that he is capable of considering at this moment. He had been about to make the same suggestion that Anspach had offered when Miller silenced him.

Teeter is capable of thinking altruistically; he simply refuses to do so. He is doing now what he generally does when faced with something unpleasant: he is looking away, as though he is distracted by something else, a tactic that seems to work almost every time.

It is Asher whose thoughts would shock everyone if the group had the collective acumen to see beneath the reserved exterior, the impassive and inexpressive face. Something that Miller said a few moments ago has forced him into an intense introspection.

Asher has learned, over the course of his long professional life, that there occasionally comes a time for many men when they are faced with the necessity to make a decision and take a course of action that they just don't see coming. They are driven, usually through no fault of their own, to wrestle between *self* and *other* in ways that are starkly laid out for them. Their initial impulse is to defer these times, and the decisions they call for, until later, with the hope that the necessity for commitment might disappear. They experience anger at the unfairness of being placed in a position that makes it necessary. They experience the pride of picturing themselves doing the right and proper thing, or they feel the self-revulsion that results from imagining otherwise. Or both.

Asher is struggling with this now. Miller said his words, and Asher was instantly struck with a sense of irony in the situation that he could not articulate if he had to. There are two things that are now being forced together in his mind that he wants to uncouple back into their separate pieces, and he is struggling mightily to find a way to do that.

The first thing is not Sanchez's bad luck, but a more specific manifestation of that misfortune. *In a little while*, Miller had said, *the shock is going to wear off, and he will be in horrible pain.*

That realization is now in brute contention with another one.

Asher has a full bottle of laudanum.

When Thomas Asher was twenty years old, he fell in love with the daughter of a neighboring rancher. This was up in Smith County, Texas, in the spring of 1880.

His father had a good-sized spread near Tyler, and Asher and his brother Gideon helped with its day-to-day running. Asher's father felt so strongly about the necessity of his sons laboring on the family business that neither of the brothers went beyond the eighth grade. This was a source of considerable tension between his parents.

The girl's name was Imogene, and Asher became so fixated on her that it kept him awake nights and prompted him to begin considering the kind of future they could make together. He had met her through the Baptist Church their father carted them off to every Sunday morning and Wednesday night. He treated her with courtesy and respect, and she responded in kind.

One night during dinner, Asher told his family of his feelings. His mother was an active Catholic who went to Mass in Tyler, so she did not know the girl at all well, except by sight. She told Asher to feel free to bring Imogene to supper on the following Saturday night. Asher looked at his father, who expressed no reservations.

And so, on the following Saturday night, Imogene Westerman came to dinner, and she and Asher sat in the parlor with his parents and had a wonderful evening. Later that night, he took her home in the buggy, and before she got out to go into the house, they kissed for the first time. Asher was euphoric.

They began to talk of marriage, and everything was perfect. One night they discussed their plans.

"Would you see us moving into the big house with your parents or building a small one to get us through until they pass?" she asked.

This question startled Asher. "Imogene, I ain't going to inherit the ranch. That goes to Gideon. He's the older brother. I will get some sort of seed money, but Dad don't want the property split up."

"Oh," Imogene said. "I didn't realize that." After a moment, she pecked him on the cheek and said, "Well, the world is our oyster."

And so, the courtship continued in that vein for several months. Imogene was over to the ranch a great deal and became almost like a family member in her own right. No date was set for a wedding; Asher wanted first to get a clear direction for his life. But it was understood by everyone that marriage was a foregone conclusion, and Asher began looking beyond the ranch for a suitable vocation.

Late one afternoon, Asher came in from the south range, tired and dirty from a day of herding strays. Imogene's horse was tethered in front, and he walked up the steps and into the large hallway. He went into the kitchen for a drink of water, and found his mother at the large stove, cooking, and crying quietly.

"What's wrong?" he asked, but she shook her head and avoided looking at him.

From the doorway, Imogene said, "Thomas, can I see you for a few minutes?" Asher followed her down the hallway into the parlor.

Gideon was there waiting for them, and Imogene walked over and sat down by *him*, took *his* hand in hers, and looked directly into Asher's eyes. She said, with only the smallest trace of regret, "Gideon and I need to talk to you." Asher realized later that he should have seen it coming.

That was thirty-five years ago, and he has never again felt the kind of anger he experienced that day. It was all-consuming for a very long time. It faded a bit as the years passed, but never really went completely away. Gideon and Imogene were married, and she bore him four sons and two daughters, before dying of diphtheria in 1906. Asher left home the month after their wedding, and except for the separate funerals for his mother and father, he has not spoken to his brother in all that time. The anger has simmered all those years. Asher does not want to relinquish his bitterness, but there are times when he does *want* to want to.

Anger of that same intensity is what Asher is feeling right now. It is coming up from the depths of some reservoir he didn't even know was there, and it is washing over him like the waters of some unnatural baptism. It forcefully surprises him, and it is so powerful that he finds himself surrendering to it and embracing it wholly.

What is this Mexican, this foul and dirty greaser, to *him*? He has no responsibility here. He did not cause the pain that is coming for the man. He has his *own* pain.

What is this shiftless old bastard even *doing* here?

What is *Asher* even doing here?

Asher stands by the sorrel, looking down at the bare ground, and the only way any of the other men would be able to gauge his anger would be to note the muscles of his temple flexing, and the intense fixity of his gaze as he frantically processes his thoughts.

We need to continue the search, Miller is saying, but Asher isn't listening. Asher knows instinctively the right thing to do, and he is desperately casting about for an alternative.

He wants to satisfy both his wrath and his *conscience*.

Asher could not care less about the Mexican and his pain, but there is something in the recesses of his being that he *does* care about. He does not want to do anything that could later lead to possible *guilt*.

Asher has faith, after a fashion, and he has often wondered about the relationship of it to conscience. He believes in conscience because he has felt deeply the guilt of his transgressions. That is why, ten years ago, he submitted to the washing away of his sins, and a new life in Christ Jesus. He has never completely *felt* that new life in Christ Jesus, but he still feels the guilt of his transgressions, and he wonders, not for the first time, which derives from which?

His laudanum means much more to him than it should. In fact, it means everything to him. He doesn't think that Beulah understands how much he has come to depend on it. It holds him now in a paralyzing vise. The pain of his busted back is one thing, and the laudanum helps that. But the pain of no laudanum, in and of itself, is more than he thinks he can bear.

Why is he wrestling with this? Why should he increase his own pain to alleviate the suffering of a man he does not even know? Who is this man to him? Is it at all possible that allowing this man to die an agonizing death, when he could assuage it, has no more moral significance than shooting a rattlesnake? Asher's need for the laudanum is so great that he finds himself caring more about getting his next sip of laudanum than he does about almost anything else in the world.

I know that's cold, Miller is saying, *but there it is. Cold?* If Miller wants *cold*, Asher can give him *cold*.

Asher looks up at Miller, and at the men standing there, and then past them to a landscape that offers no solace whatsoever. Asher's emotions are so clouded that they place a dark filter over every perception coming into him. He wonders if the laudanum is causing this.

He realizes now that he isn't going to find any moral clarity right at this moment, and that there isn't time to thrash this all out before what is happening in front of him has to be resolved. He knows that if he rides away, he will lock himself into a lifetime of regret, and a self-loathing well beyond what he already feels. He needs time. He just needs a little more *time*.

The Mexican is lying there, back to him, and the fact that Asher cannot see his face makes his ambivalence easier. He is thinking that, at the very least, he could give the greaser just enough of the laudanum to salve his conscience. But he can't do that in front of the others.

I need a volunteer to stay with him, Miller is saying.

"I'll do it," Asher says.

4

Sometimes, it has been Miller's experience that when a difficult moment has immediately passed, and a deeper difficulty still lies ahead, a lethargy will begin to take hold of him, and any possibility of forward movement becomes almost beyond comprehension.

Miller feels that now. He has picked up his map and put it back into his coat pocket, and he stands next to his horse, one hand on the horn of the saddle, regarding Asher's worn face. Miller does not want to be here, in this terrible place, at this terrible time. He does not want to be in Duval County, pursuing men who probably don't exist for reasons that almost certainly have no value. He does not even want particularly to be in Texas, and he is sorry now that he looked for some measure of redemption for his presence at Bud Dajo with the Texas Rangers. He had thought that the quest for atonement was behind him.

What he *does* want is to be home with Leona, sitting at the dining room table, telling her what is happening, and waiting for her exquisite soul to help him determine what to do. But Leona is not here; she is back in Laredo, and Miller has to deal with the here-and-now. He has made a decision, and he must now take action.

He may have told the men that Sanchez has only a few hours of life, but he doesn't really know that, not for sure. Certainly, the poor wretch is dying, but he may linger for a while. Miller is still wedded to the idea that putting the old man on a horse would be cruel. Even if he could get Sanchez to a doctor alive, the pain the old man would suffer would be for nothing. It is a fatal wound; Miller is quite sure of that.

He realizes that he is continuing with the search because he cannot bear to be here and watch the old man die in front of him. He could half-convince himself that continuing the search might be legitimate, but his heart knows better. Anspach's suggestion for all of them to stay with the Mexican was, he knows, the only righteous course of action. But no amount of guilt can dissuade him from avoiding the emotional agony of watching this play out. He is shocked that Asher has offered to stay; he had been about to order Anspach to do it.

Miller now forces his mind to identify and act on the immediate priority: he needs to leave Asher with some provisions.

Miller turns to Teeter and says, "We're leaving one of the pack mules. I want you to unload everything and split it into two sections. Separate one-third of the food and any medical supplies that might be there and leave them on the ground. Put everything else on the pack mule with the better legs. What else do we have?"

"Frying pan. Extra bedroll. Such like that," Teeter says.

"Take them with us," Miller says.

He is now thinking of exactly how he should tell Asher to proceed. There are so many contingencies, all of them based on how long the old man will linger, that Miller tries to break them down into the fewest number of possibilities.

He looks at Asher and is surprised at the complete indifference that he sees, at how so completely apathetic Asher seems. He walks over to him and stands facing him, his back to Sanchez and Anspach, and says, "This may take a little while. The old man, I mean."

"I'll be here until it's over," Asher says.

"Well, thank you for doing this," Miller says. Asher says nothing. "I think that this will give you excellent leverage with Moates," Miller says, and Asher again has no response. His expression is a cipher.

"I doubt that we have anything with us that is going to help his pain," Miller says. "Have you ever been with a dying man?"

Asher shakes his head. "Not like this."

"Well, it's going to get very bad, very quickly. I wish I knew what to tell you." And now a thought comes to him, something that has until now been simmering in the back of his mind. "You know, sometimes you can find yourself in a position to do something that you *need* to do, that you might not normally be able to."

Asher's face turns dark. "You need to spell that out," he says.

Miller's face reddens. He hesitates and then says, "I am just saying that you're going to be out here by yourself, and sometimes the most merciful thing to do . . ."

"You go straight to hell," Asher says. "I won't do it."

But even as Asher says this, part of him is wondering if he can be so emphatic about this because he knows he has the laudanum. Would he be the paragon of virtue if he didn't have it? He looks at Miller and softens a little. "I could never do that," he says.

Miller nods and is so upset with himself for having suggested it that, in his shame, he looks away from Asher, avoiding eye contact. He walks back a few steps.

"Well," he says, "if he dies before dark, just go ahead on to Falfurrias like you were going to. Take the train back to Laredo. If it is tomorrow, go north to San Diego and rendezvous with us there, if you can." He glances back to Asher, who nods.

There is a question lingering, but Asher does not want to ask it, because he doesn't want to be bound by the answer. He waits for Miller to address it. But Miller doesn't get the chance to be proactive about it, because Teeter suddenly asks, "What about the shovel? Does it stay or go?"

Miller looks back at Asher now, and their eyes lock, and he suddenly feels a moral vacuum deep within himself. He wants to say, "It goes with *us*," but that is not what he says. He wants to apologize for the terrible suggestion that he made to Asher a moment ago, but that is not what he does. He wants to feel whole and clean, and above reproach, but that is not what he feels. Instead, he looks at Asher and hopes that perhaps the decision won't have to be his. But that is not to be.

"You need to answer him," Asher says.

A moment passes, while Miller wrestles with his conscience. He waits for Asher to say something, *anything*, but there is only silence. Finally, he says, "Leave it," and now his self-loathing is complete. He and Asher regard each other for a moment, and then Miller turns away.

Ten minutes later, Teeter has finished, and Miller can think of nothing left to do or say. He walks over to Sanchez and regards him for a moment. The old man is in a fetal position, eyes closed, breathing shallowly.

"I think he's passed out," Anspach says.

Miller is relieved because he does not want to go through the anguish of having to use Anspach to apologize to the old man for what has happened.

"Let's mount up," he says.

"Shouldn't we pray over him?" Anspach asks.

"Of course," Miller says, embarrassed yet again. "Perhaps you could say a few words."

Asher has been quiet because he does not want to delay their departure. He needs some laudanum badly. But Miller's words anger him.

"*You* should be the one to pray," Asher says to Miller. "Or Burnett."

Miller looks at Asher with a glance that begs for mercy. All he wants is for this horrible moment to be over, to be riding away with all of this at his back. He has no words for prayer because he knows damned well that God could not possibly be listening to him.

He says, "Let's all just pray quietly for a moment."

So they remove their hats, and bow their heads, and stand there, waiting for someone to break the silence. Are they actually praying?

That depends on how you define it.

"Mount up," Miller says again, and they all climb onto their horses. Miller takes one last look at Asher, who is now standing over Sanchez, and then he wheels his mount and begins to lead his men to the east.

Asher stands and watches them ride away. Even before they disappear on the far horizon, he removes the laudanum from his jacket, regards the fourth of an inch of thick fluid in the bottom of the small bottle, and downs it all in one long, magnificent draw. Then he walks over to his horse, takes his canteen, pours a little water into the bottle, and shakes it firmly, keeping his thumb over the mouth. He drinks *that* down, examines the bottle to make sure that there is not the slightest trace of the amber fluid left, and then he throws the bottle as far as he can. He then takes another swig from the canteen. After a few moments, the familiar glow begins, and both the ache and the need fade away.

Asher turns now to Sanchez, who has shifted his position a bit, and whose eyes are half-open, watching him silently. He squats down and touches the old man's shoulder and says, "You okay?"

The old man's eyes fully open and he looks at Asher's canteen and says, "*Agua, por favor.*"

Asher lifts the old man's head and puts the canteen to his lips. The Mexican takes three sips, and then turns his head away, and closes his eyes again.

It is mid-morning now, but the chill is still in the air. Asher stands up and looks down at Sanchez, and it occurs to him that if he can make the old man more comfortable, he should do it now, before the worst sets in. He looks up to find Sanchez's horse and sees it and the old man's pack mule about twenty yards away, heads down, looking for something to chew from the meager scrubland menu.

He begins to walk toward them. The mule backs away from him, but the horse remains in place, and Asher is able to simply walk up to him and take him by the halter and lead him back to join his own animals. He will deal with the pack mule later, if necessary.

He removes the saddle from Sanchez's horse and walks over to the old man. The saddle is an ancient Charro, and the weathered leather is soft and supple. He lays it gently on the ground by the old man's head, then walks back to the horse to get a bedroll, only to discover that there is not one there. It seems that he will deal with the pack mule sooner, then. It takes about fifteen minutes to walk the stubborn animal down, and then another twenty minutes to cajole and prod it over to the other animals. In case it bolts again, Asher removes everything from the mule, except the halter, and lays it out on the ground. During this entire time, he keeps a wary eye on the sleeping Mexican.

He takes the dirty bedroll over and lays it next to the saddle, and then goes back and removes his own saddle from the sorrel and brings it over so that he has something to sit on. While he waits for Sanchez to rouse again, he takes his first close look at him.

The old man could be seventy, or eighty. Or sixty. His face reflects a hard life, a life of deprivation. And, it seems to Asher, a life of alcohol. It is there, etched into his face, that abstract, indefinable *something*: the deeply creased lines, the mottled splotches of pink, the slightly bulbous nose. Yes. This man is a serious drinker.

What else? The clothes are ragged and dirty. The once-vibrant colors of the serape have long ago faded to a faint pastel, and it has obviously not been washed in many years, if ever. The stains of fresh blood on the front of it are the brightest part of it. His sandals have all but worn away, and Asher can see the dirty feet, with their toenails almost as broken and filthy as the man's fingernails. Asher begins to sense that this man is one of the dregs of society, an outcast, even in what Asher has always regarded to be a relatively uncivilized culture.

No doubt about it, the man is simply distasteful to look at, ugly in fact, in that in-bred peasant way. There are good Mexicans, to be sure, but Asher has always considered them to be generally a coarse people.

Asher finds all of this reassuring. He feels that it somehow lessens any fixed obligations. It allows him to believe that the old man's death will be no great tragedy, as it would be if it were a child, or a woman, or a decent and productive citizen. It allows the old man to merit, in Asher's mind, something less than a full measure of pity and compassion.

There is a small commotion from the animals, and Asher's attention is shifted away. Two of the horses are engaged in a gentle head-butting for access to a tuft of sparse vegetation. When Asher's gaze moves back, the old man is looking at him.

"*Hola,*" Asher says. He starts to smile but then checks himself almost immediately. He does not want to convey cheerfulness to a dying man. That would seem . . . *rude.*

The old man's head is lying on his left arm, and he attempts to raise it so that he can shift position. As he does, a moan comes, somewhat loud, and belly-deep.

"Here we go," Asher says to himself, under his breath.

Asher moves forward, off his saddle, into a kneeling position beside the old man. He lifts Sanchez's head a bit, reaches over with his other hand and pulls the saddle toward them, and then lowers the old man's head back down on it, turning him over on his back as he does so. The man's legs involuntarily draw up, but he does seem to find some relief in the new position.

Asher notices as he touches him directly that the old man is shivering. The chill has left the morning air, but it is still March, so the temperature is still relatively brisk and will remain so. Asher takes the dirty bedroll and spreads it out on a level piece of earth next to Sanchez, and then pulls back the top.

"Let's get warm," Asher says, and reaches down, and the Mexican raises his right arm and drapes it around Asher's neck. Asher reaches under the old man's knees with one arm and under his back with the other, and then half-lifts and half-drags him toward the bedroll.

They both moan. The pain, which has stayed subdued because of the large swig of the opiate he has swallowed, wells up suddenly from Asher's lower back, and he all but drops the Mexican onto the bedroll.

"Son of a bitch," Asher says loudly, and bends over and places his right arm behind his back and presses his clenched fist against his lower spine, as though this will do any good. He is now on his knees, bent over until his head almost touches the ground. He looks over to the old man directly, and curses.

But Sanchez is enduring a great deal of pain. His hands are pressed to his stomach, and his eyes are clenched shut. "*Madre de Dios,*" he says and begins to weep.

Asher waits for his *own* pain to subside as he listens to the Mexican's slowly escalating whimpering next to him. After a moment, the pain dulls enough for him to get back into a kneeling position, and he reaches over and pulls the top of the bedroll over Sanchez. Then he slowly stands up, waits another moment for the pain to lessen a bit more, and bends over and puts the saddle back under the old man's head.

The time he has been dreading has arrived.

"I will be right back," he says, mostly to himself because he does not think that the Mexican can understand him. He walks slowly over to the horses and takes the sorrel by the halter and then opens the right-side saddlebag. From it, he removes the unopened bottle of laudanum, enveloped in the red rag he had wrapped it in almost thirty hours ago. He carries it, still wrapped, back over to Sanchez; he does not want to risk dropping the bottle on the hard ground. He kneels on one knee next to Sanchez and then allows himself to shift over into a sitting position. He hesitates for just a moment, cementing his resolve.

Finally, he holds the bottle up and says to Sanchez, "Hey, amigo, look at this." Sanchez opens his eyes and his gaze goes to the small bottle, and he immediately understands what it is.

"Manna from heaven," Asher says.

Asher pries out the new cork, raises the bottle to his lips, and takes a sip. He waits a moment, and then smiles for Sanchez, even before the relief actually begins. He wants Sanchez to understand.

Still moaning, the old man is watching him with interest. Asher reaches down, cradles the back of the sweaty head, and lifts it gently toward him. He then puts the mouth of the bottle carefully to the Mexican's lips and tilts it gently.

The old man starts to gulp greedily, as though it is a bottle of tequila, and Asher pulls it back quickly. "No, no, no," Asher says. "Sip it. *Sip* it." He brings the bottle back to his own lips and kisses it, to demonstrate the restraint he desires. The old man nods, and Asher lowers the bottle again to his lips. Asher lets him take a sip and then pulls the bottle away.

Asher's glow is starting now, and he looks at the bottle and puts the cork back in it. Sanchez is still moaning, and Asher watches him carefully, to see if the amount he allowed the old man is going to be sufficient.

It pleases Asher to hear the old man's moaning begin to wane, and after a few minutes, they stop altogether, and the old man, who has been returning Asher's gaze, actually smiles a little.

"*Bueno*," he whispers. "*Bueno*." Then, "*Gracias. Gracias.*" He closes his eyes and drifts slowly back into unconsciousness.

Asher looks down at the laudanum bottle, and he sees that about a half-inch of the fluid has been consumed. He begins now the inevitable calculations in his mind: the estimates of what is left that will be recalibrated after every consumption. He will always end these appraisals by converting the remaining volume to *time*.

It is a four-inch bottle, so he quickly estimates that there are seven remaining doses for the two of them. He knows from experience that the duration between each dose will last a shorter amount of time than the one before it. He begins to wonder if the laudanum might run out before Sanchez takes his final breath. He rewraps the bottle carefully.

He glances back to Sanchez again and now, for the first time since the accident, Asher wonders about the old man's wound. Should he do something to it? Asher knows very little about field doctoring, particularly with this kind of wound. If he had any alcohol, he might clean it. But to what purpose? Surely death will come before advanced infection.

And then it occurs to him further that he hasn't seen much blood.

He slides over and carefully lifts the old man's serape and is startled to see how much blood has congealed beneath it. He imagines that if he turns the old man over, there will be an equal amount on the other side. He glances down to himself and notices that the front of his coat has now been smeared with it and he is suddenly angry because he knows that Beulah will not be able to get it completely out. He curses under his breath.

He watches for a while Sanchez's measured, labored breathing and he begins to consider the possibility that Sanchez might live through the day. He wonders if they should have gone ahead and made him endure a horse for the possibility of getting him to a doctor.

The sun reaches its apogee and starts down again to the western horizon. The old man is quiet, but Asher knows that will not last. He sits quietly, calmed by the utter stillness of the moment. He is afraid that any movement will hasten the return of his own pain.

After a while, the old man begins to stir, and then the low moans begin again, and Sanchez opens his eyes and looks around, and then his gaze settles on Asher. His hands move again to his stomach, and his legs start to draw up. Asher is unsure about how much time has passed since the first dose of laudanum. He supposes it to have been about an hour, and he resolves on this go-around to time it. He reaches into his vest pocket and pulls out his watch. It is half-past one.

Asher reaches down and picks up the red rag and unwraps the laudanum. Again, he takes a sip himself and then helps Sanchez. The old man smacks his lips and then, despite his pain, shuts his eyes and patiently waits for relief. Asher looks at the bottle. A quarter of it is gone: six more doses for them; six or seven more hours.

A cold despondency begins to come over him.

After a few minutes, Sanchez again dozes off, and Asher decides that he needs to get his own bedroll and prepare a fire for the evening, while he can still easily find the odd scraps of dry brushwood, and while the laudanum in his own body is still working from the latest dose. He rises painfully to his feet and spends half an hour walking in a circle around their camp, picking up stray sticks, and stacking them neatly between his saddle and Sanchez's bedroll. Finally, he decides that he has enough to get them through the night, if it comes to that.

Next, he goes to the sorrel and removes his bedroll, and then brings it back over and lays it down next to his saddle. He is not hungry, and he cannot imagine developing an appetite while the old man still lives. But he walks back again anyway and surveys all of the supplies that Teeter has left haphazardly strewn on the ground. Rather than do triage on them, he simply makes a half dozen trips to move it all over to where he and the old man reside. He stacks it all close by.

Asher sits back down on his saddle. His back is shot, but he waits.

At 2:40 consciousness returns to Sanchez, and his pain returns with it. Asher again uncorks the laudanum, but this time, instead of going first, he begins to administer it to Sanchez.

A curious thing happens.

The old man, though obviously hurting, shakes his head and raises his finger to point to Asher. "*Voya primero,*" he says, and it occurs to Asher that the old man is, in some gesture of propriety, insisting that Asher sips first. This touches him. Asher takes his sip and only then does the old man indulge. He then lays his head back and says, "*Gracias,*" but this time he does not immediately drop back into sleep.

For the first time, the old man seems to be taking notice of what is around them. Asher watches his gaze as it takes in the bedroll he sleeps in, and the distant horses, still grazing, and then the stack of dry wood ready for the evening.

"*Muy bien,*" he says and offers a small nod and then a smile.

His gaze now shifts to the supplies, and as he looks at them, a frown suddenly appears on his weathered face.

"*No,*" he says. "*No, por favor.*" He looks back to Asher, and his face is quickly moving beyond apprehension toward a full panic. "*Eso no,*" he pleads.

Asher looks over to the supplies and cannot imagine what is agitating the Mexican. Finding nothing that justifies the old man's reaction, he begins to look at each item, one-by-one, and it suddenly becomes clear to him what the old man sees.

The shovel.

Asher, shaken by the old man's distress, glances back to him, but what he sees suddenly is not Sanchez, but *himself*, as the old man must see *him*, and he sees himself using the shovel to put the body into the earth, *to be forgotten*. For the first time, he becomes aware of what the old man must be experiencing, not just at this moment, but everything since the shooting, and Asher is suddenly filled with a deep remorse.

Asher does not know what he is going to do when the old man dies, but he wants desperately to end the old man's fear, to reassure him. The only thing that he can immediately think of to do is to rise, move over to the supplies, and pick up the shovel. He throws it into the distance with as much strength as he can muster, pain be damned. He turns back to Sanchez, who is nodding with understanding.

"You're going home," Asher says.

5

O nly later will Beulah Asher come to regret some of what she includes in her confession, and some of what she leaves out.

It is Thursday morning, and she is working on a dress in her little sewing shop off the alley when she becomes aware of someone standing in the doorway. She looks up and sees a handsome woman of perhaps thirty-five, regarding her with some curiosity.

"Mrs. Asher?" the woman says. "I am Leona Miller. I have come to ask you a question." And now Beulah knows that Teeter has talked, sometime during the interval between their room and the train depot.

"I understand," Beulah says evenly, with no hesitation whatsoever. "Would you like me to tell you everything?"

"Yes, I *would* like that," Leona Miller says. "Very much."

"Please sit down," Beulah says.

And this is the story she tells:

Beulah Steinkamp was born in July of 1868 in Macoupin County, Illinois. She was the fourth of nine children born to an alcoholic share-cropper and his wife, a consumptive woman who Beulah would later remember only for her perpetual sadness. When Beulah was nine, her mother finally grew tired of an abused, hardscrabble existence and hanged herself, for her husband and all the children to see, on a large, beautiful oak tree within sight of the decrepit farmhouse they called home. Her father expressed little surprise and even less grief. He never remarried, and his drinking grew unchecked.

Beulah lost her virginity to her father before she was thirteen years old. The family was not churched, and her father allowed very little con-tact with the world, so she had no way of verifying her suspicion that this was not the normal way of things. Indeed, when one of her younger sisters grew old enough to attract their father's interest, Beulah was re-lieved for his diminished expectations of *her*. It was many years before she began to slowly develop any guilt for this reaction.

"My God," Leona Miller says, sitting back in her chair and raising her right hand to her white throat. She is pale with shock. "This sort of thing actually happens?"

"Mrs. Miller," Beulah says, "this world is not what it is supposed to be."

When she was sixteen, Beulah caught the eye of a farm-to-farm plow salesman named Harvey Weintraub, who was twenty years her senior. Two days after meeting him, she left her home in the middle of the night, and she and Weintraub were married by a justice of the peace in a perfunctory ceremony that made her happier than she had ever been.

This happiness lasted for three weeks. Weintraub took her to his tenement rooms in Chicago, and Beulah quickly found that she had merely traded one abusive inebriate for another. But she was sixteen years old and had no place else to go, so she endured it as stoically as she could. A month after her seventeenth birthday, she discovered that she was with child. She was less than thrilled.

In the seventh month of her pregnancy, her husband returned home from a poker game that had not gone well. He was drunk, and when Beulah asked him where they would get money for the rent, already past due, he became enraged and beat her so severely that she had to be taken to the hospital. She lost the baby, and she was told then that there would be no more children.

A police detective came to her bed in the indigent ward to get a statement, and Beulah was, at first, reluctant to give the details. But the cop, a big, blustery man named Collins, kept pressing.

"He should not get away with this," he said. "If you press charges, we can have him locked up for quite a spell."

"I ain't got no place else to go," Beulah said. "No place."

Collins looked at her, as if for the first time, and said, "I know someone who could help you. Take you in. Get you on your feet."

"Who would help someone like *me*?"

"My brother and his wife," Collins said. "Helping young women like you is something they do all the time."

Beulah considered this for a moment and said, "I would appreciate any help I can get. But I still don't want to do nothing against my husband." She was thinking that if she didn't anger him further, she could always return to him if she ended up with nothing better.

To her surprise, Collins agreed immediately, and the next day he brought his brother Richard and sister-in-law Maisie to the ward. They were nicer to her than anyone had ever been in her life. They took her with them that very day, after paying the medical bills, and that night she slept in a guest bedroom in their fine home, in a canopied bed so wondrous she felt like a queen. The day after that, they took her to a nice residence on the outskirts of Chicago, where she was introduced to four other young women who were in the same straits as Beulah.

For the next month, she mended physically and ate well. Maisie Collins would come most afternoons to talk, and Beulah found herself sharing everything about her past. She was grateful beyond anything she had ever felt for the affection and care she was receiving.

"How wonderful people can be," Leona Miller says.

"People can *be wonderful," Beulah replies. "But not the people that you first think are. Never. Not in my case, anyway."*

One day, the Collinses came by the house and took Beulah to

lunch in one of the fine restaurants on the shore of Lake Michigan that cater to people much farther above her station than *she* could ever hope to be. Afterward, they walked slowly along the delicate, tree-lined concourse and sat down on one of the benches.

"Beulah," Richard Collins said, "Maisie and I have something to discuss with you, a business proposition. After you hear us out, you have the freedom to say no, and there will be no resentment on our part. What we have done for you has nothing to do with any expectations, except for what might be best for you."

Beulah looked over at Maisie, who sat with a smile so warm and loving that Beulah could not imagine what the proposal could be.

"I am a businessman, Beulah," Collins continued, "and I have a variety of investments. One of these businesses is a social club on the lower east side, that caters to a very special clientele."

"I don't understand," Beulah said.

"You are a very attractive young woman," Collins said. "You should use that to your advantage while you still can."

"I don't understand," Beulah said.

"I want you to join the staff there. You will find it a very comfortable existence. You will be well-compensated. You will be taught all the necessary skills, and you will be brought in gradually. I will secure your divorce, and you can leave any time you like. It will be a way for you to build a nest-egg for the next phase in your life, after that."

Beulah looked at Maisie, who was still smiling and beaming with anticipation of Beulah's reaction, and then back to Collins.

"I understand," Beulah said.

"And you accepted?" Leona Miller asks. She is incredulous.

"Yes, I did," Beulah says. "I did not even hesitate. What did I know? It was a direction for me, for the first time in my life. What do you think? That I had something inside me that said this was wrong? I did not."

"Yes, you did." Leona Miller is nodding emphatically. "It is there for all of us. Call it conscience, or whatever you like. But it is there."

"Well, if it is there," Beulah says, "someone has to show it to you. Nobody is going to find it on their own. No one ever showed me."

Leona Miller is quiet at this, and Beulah says, "Mrs. Miller, I am not attempting to defend myself here. I obviously see things now that I did not see then. But if you are going to judge me, don't judge my decision right there, at the beginning. Judge me on what comes after."

In the late summer of 1886, just after her eighteenth birthday, Beulah Weintraub went to work at the Constabulary Club, a four-story brownstone on Constitution Avenue, luxuriously appointed and immaculate, and finer than any place that she had ever imagined. She was one of a stable of twenty women, all attractive, who ranged in age from eighteen to forty-six. They were good to her, patient and kind, and she grew to regard them as older sisters. They taught her the skills she needed, social and otherwise, along with hygiene and technique. She was educated in the arts of diction and grammar. She ate well, had her own fine room, and she worked five nights a week, and Saturdays from mid-afternoon. She was allowed, actually encouraged, to sleep late, when she would rise, have a well-prepared lunch, and then an afternoon of leisure. She was well-paid and, for the most part, she enjoyed the work. The Constabulary Club was elite, with a carefully cultivated and moderated clientele, so it avoided most of the problems of a lower-class brothel.

In short, for six years, life seemed good.

Any prostitute worth her wages develops, over time, a set of repeat customers, and Beulah was no exception. One of these customers was an earnest young man named Jasper Woodbine. He was the assistant branch manager at a mercantile bank on the loop, and over the course of a year, he fell in love with Beulah. She could see it happening and thought about discouraging him as gently as she could, but he was a very nice man, and she did not want to hurt him. Or lose his business. One night, before their session even started, he proposed.

"Jasper, I like you very much," she explained to him. "But I do not think I *love* you."

"That doesn't matter," Woodbine replied. "That could come in time. Look, I have been given an important assignment. I have been promoted to the branch manager position of a mercantile bank in El Paso, Texas. I want to take you with me."

"I will have to think about it," Beulah said, and the next day she related the conversation to a few of the other girls.

"Take it," said Sally, perhaps her closest friend. "Take it *now*. He's a *banker*, for God's sake. Dream come true."

So she took it. She left the Constabulary Club, and married Jasper Woodbine in a Methodist service on the north side, with his parents and friends and several hundred well-wishers in attendance: clergy and judges and politicians and bankers, at least a dozen of whom she knew carnally. She moved into his apartment on the North Shore until he finished an apprenticeship. For those six weeks, she stayed mainly in the apartment, to avoid running into any more clients of the Club.

In May of 1892, Jasper and Beulah Woodbine moved to El Paso, once a wild frontier town of some reputation, but now a thriving city at the center of the cattle business. The mercantile bank Jasper managed had been there for ten years and was well-established.

Beulah was quite surprised and pleased to see how easily Jasper integrated into El Paso business society, and Jasper himself was quite surprised at how easily he was accepted. Beulah began to see in him a change, as he evolved from his natural reticence and began to exhibit a degree of independence that she had never imagined was there.

They lived for six years in an upper-middle-class home that pleased Beulah very much. They had enough money to live well, and Jasper was a very agreeable companion. In time, she grew to love him, after a fashion. They attended a Methodist church near the city center, where Beulah taught Sunday School, and Jasper was on the board.

But something began to gnaw at her husband, and it started with their home. "I am a bank manager, for God's sake," he said to her over dinner one night. "Our home does not adequately reflect that status. I am going to ask for a serious raise. They owe it to me."

A month later, they purchased a small mansion four blocks from the country club, as well as a membership at the club itself. Then a steady progression of new things began to be delivered: fine things, including furniture and art.

And so, for ten years they lived well. Beulah often wondered about how much money Jasper earned, but he always lightly deflected her questions, so she relaxed about it.

One morning in the spring of 1908, he left for work, and she kissed him good-bye at the door. At mid-afternoon, their maid came out to the backyard where Beulah was gardening and brought with her two men, who showed her their city police badges. They were looking for her husband.

Her world came undone.

Jasper Woodbine had gone to work that morning in his usual good, expansive mood, and was shocked to find, on his arrival at the bank, the presence of the senior auditor from the mercantile exchange in Chicago, who brusquely told him that he was there to examine the books, with no delay. Woodbine took him into his office and shut the door, and the bank staff could hear raised voices. After half an hour, Woodbine emerged from the office, took his hat, and announced that he had a business appointment and that the auditor was not to be disturbed. By early afternoon he had not returned, and when the assistant manager opened the door of his office, he found the auditor on the floor, with a crushed skull, next to a bloodied marble bookend.

Jasper Woodbine had grabbed $400 in cash and boarded the first train out of town. He was apprehended ten days later, in Blanchard, Oklahoma, attempting to cash a fraudulent cashier's check.

Beulah was destroyed. Everything they owned had been dishonestly obtained, and she left the house, and the city, in abject disgrace, once she was able to convince the prosecutor of her complete innocence, a process that took six weeks, and finished crushing her spirits.

Jasper Woodbine waived extradition, and a Texas Ranger named Thomas Asher was sent to Oklahoma to bring Woodbine back to El Paso for trial. Woodbine was tried for murder three months later and sentenced to hang at the penitentiary in Huntsville.

During the long train trip back to El Paso, Woodbine and Asher talked. They were as relaxed and casual as two handcuffed men can be. Woodbine told Asher of his regret for all that this meant for his wife. He asked Asher to please arrange a visit between them.

Once the trial was concluded, and Woodbine had been transferred to Huntsville, Asher dutifully searched for her, and a month later he found her sequestered in the home of friends on the south side of San Antonio. He could not have explained to anyone why he went to this much trouble; somewhere along the line, his compassion transferred from Woodbine, whom Asher liked, to his wife, whom he had never before met and who was soon to be an undeserving widow. He was able to take her to Huntsville two weeks before Woodbine was executed. Asher admired her for her composure, but her spirit was clearly broken.

At Woodbine's request, Asher was in attendance when he dropped through the trap door into eternity. They had talked and prayed in the holding cell in the hours leading up to his death, and Woodbine's last words were to thank Asher for his kindness.

That night, Asher took Beulah for a quiet walk. She was disconsolate. He told her of Woodbine's love for her and relayed to her everything that her husband had asked him to say to her after he was gone. She said little, and he found himself grieving as much for her as for Woodbine. "Is there anything I can do?" he asked, and she shook her head. "Do you need money?" he asked, and she shook her head. "Can I help you in any way?" he asked, and she shook her head.

He took her back to her hotel and said good-bye to her at the door. It was one of the saddest nights of his life.

Asher is never able to explain to Beulah's satisfaction what it was that prompted him to go looking for her after four years. He tells her of his loneliness and his desire for companionship. He tells her of the thoughts he would have of her from time to time, and the visual memory of her standing in the doorway of her hotel. He admits to her that he wanted to spend his years with someone grateful to him for loving her. What he never explains, but which Beulah nevertheless understands, is the overwhelming compassion he felt for her.

One simmering Sunday afternoon in the summer of 1913, he awoke in his room after a nap and realized that he was tired of being alone. Beulah Woodbine suddenly became the center of his thoughts. The next morning, he went into Render Moates' office and announced that he wanted to take several weeks of his accumulated leave time.

He had no idea where to start looking for her; her friends in San Antonio had lost touch. That afternoon, he boarded a train for El Paso.

He went to the bank that Woodbine had embezzled from, but the current manager had no idea what happened to her. Stumped, Asher considered his next step in the confinement of his hotel room, and it occurred to him that he might start with her old neighbors. The next morning, he went to the local newspaper office and found the articles covering the crime and the trial. One of them supplied the address he was looking for, and that afternoon he walked the nine blocks to a lovely two-story Victorian home in an upscale neighborhood, near the country club. The woman who answered the door was unable to help.

He knocked on every door on both sides of the street, and politely explained who he was looking for, but at the end of the afternoon, he still had nothing. At the hotel that night, he considered his options again and realized that he had one final alternative.

In the middle of the afternoon on the following day, he arrived in Huntsville and went directly to the prison, where his self-made Ranger's badge got him into the presence of the warden very quickly. He explained what he was looking for, and the warden considered things and then shrugged. "The only thing I could suggest would be to see what happened to the body after execution." They went down to a large records room in the bowels of the building and pulled Woodbine's file.

"Didn't get a state burial," the warden said. "Body was picked up by Hatcher and Hatcher. After that, there's nothing."

By the end of the afternoon, Asher was speaking to the senior Hatcher in a small, cluttered office. "I remember that fella," the old man said. "His wife made the arrangements." Again, a file was pulled, and as he paged through it, more details emerged. "She put half down and promised the other half within ninety days. I wouldn't normally do that, but her situation was pretty sad." The old man flipped the page again and announced, "She paid it in full, too."

"Did she leave a forwarding address?" Asher said.

"Sure did," the old man replied, and he grabbed a slip of paper from a desk drawer and wrote on it, "Beulah Woodbine, 2970 Constitution Avenue, Chicago, Illinois."

Two mornings later, Asher found himself in the foyer of the Constabulary Club, quietly digesting the fact that he was standing in a glorified whorehouse. Asher came close at that moment to walking away, but something held him in place.

"I am sorry," the house madam said to him, "but she is no longer at this establishment. She left our employment several years ago."

"And you have no idea where she went?"

The woman paused and said, "She had to leave some personal items here. She said that when she got settled someplace else that she would send for them."

"And did she?"

She paused again and said, "Yes, several months later. I no longer have the address, but she had us send her things to Odessa, Texas."

Three nights later, Asher stood in the parlor of the finest brothel in Odessa and said to the madam, "I am looking for a woman named Beulah Woodbine." He opened his coat so that she could see his badge.

She nodded and said, "Her working name here is Belle. At this moment, she is with a client. Can you wait for a little while?"

So Asher sat down on a divan in the hallway, well away from the transactions occurring in the drawing room on the other side of the foyer, and wondered what the hell he was doing there. He waited, very self-consciously, and felt a peculiar mixture of revulsion *for* and envy *of* those who could relax in such a place as this.

After forty minutes, Beulah Woodbine came into the hallway, walked over to him, and said tentatively, "You wanted to see me?" She was a little softer and grayer, but otherwise unchanged. Asher stood up and stepped forward under one of the electric wall lamps. He watched her realize that she knew him from somewhere, and then he watched her search her memory, and then he watched her as it came to her.

"Asher," she said. She was astonished.

"Shame on you," Asher said, and then felt immediate regret when tears came to her eyes. She looked down at the floor, and then away.

"And shame on *me*," Asher said, "for letting this happen to you."

Beulah looked back up at Asher in misted bafflement. "It hardly *happened* to me," she said. "I just did not see any other course."

Asher was quiet for a moment, and Beulah would never know from his unreadable face the turmoil within him. After a moment he said, against every instinct he had, "I am fifty-three years old, and I ain't got a pot to piss in. I got a cheap room in a hotel in Laredo, and forty dollars in the bank. But if you want to walk away from this, and be faithful, I would like for you to be my wife."

Beulah was dumbfounded by this. She remembered his kindness to Jasper, and his graciousness to her the night of his execution. She regarded him for a moment, her mind in a cascading rush.

Finally, she said, ever so tentatively, "This profession takes a toll. I am not clean. I hope that you understand what I am saying to you."

"I do," Asher replied. He had already considered this on the long train ride from Chicago. "That just ain't important to me," he said.

She was quiet again for the longest moment in Asher's life, and then she said, against every instinct she had, "Yes."

They were married by a Baptist Minister in Laredo three days later, immediately after her full-immersion baptism in the Rio Grande.

"He told me he wanted me white as snow," Beulah is explaining to Leona Miller. "Insisted on the baptism first."

"He needed love that much?" Leona asks Beulah, amazed.

"Not just that," Beulah replies. "Thomas doesn't *need* love so much. He was looking for someone *to* love. *That's* what matters most to him."

Leona is quiet for a moment. Then she stands and extends her hand. "Thank you for your directness, Mrs. Asher," she says, with all sincerity. "I don't know what difference I can make, people being what they are, but I will talk to my husband, and do everything I can, in action and in prayer." They shake hands, and then she turns and leaves.

Beulah watches her departure without standing up because she isn't really in the present now. Her mind has drifted back to their wedding night, and something that Asher said to her that turned her way of considering herself upside down. She replays the memory in her mind.

She is standing in front of him and, before she lowers her nightdress for the first time, she says to him, "If you need time for the stench on me to wear off, I would understand."

"Don't need to wear off," Asher says. "It's all been washed away."

She thinks she understands, but she looks at him quizzically.

"In the river," Asher says.

6

Greatly allaying the old man's fears about the shovel now allows Asher to again retrieve the laudanum bottle.

He sits back on the saddle and unwraps the bottle from the rag. He regards it for a moment, and he is surprised to see that the three-fourths of the laudanum that remains does not seem to be as much as it did when he wrapped the bottle a little over an hour ago. It is not that any has been consumed, but some difference in the way he is perceiving it causes him to stop and think, and he realizes that the reason for this perception is right there in plain sight.

Asher does not want to run out of the laudanum before the old man dies. He also does not want to run out of the laudanum because of his *own* self, but that is secondary. He thinks of this realization as virtuous, until he considers it more deeply.

One Sunday afternoon in Laredo, when Asher and Beulah were

coming back from a baptism down at the river, they had seen a diseased and emaciated dog chained to a large tree in front of a shack on the edge of town. It was in obvious distress. Beulah started to pause, but Asher had taken her elbow and gently nudged her on.

"It ain't our dog," he had told her. He knew how prickly some men can get when challenged on such things.

That night in their room, he looked up from his Bible and saw that Beulah was staring out the window, lost in thought.

"What's eating at you?" he asked.

"I was just thinking about that poor animal we saw today," she said. "I feel bad about just leaving it there like that."

"Why is it so important to you?"

"Because I don't think I can bear the guilt if I don't do something."

"Then you'd be doing something for *you*, and not the dog," Asher said. He used this piece of sophistry not because he actually believed it, but because he just didn't have the energy or inclination to do anything.

Beulah frowned at this and let the matter drop.

Is this the case here? Is he fooling himself by considering that the Mexican's need comes first? Why did he even offer to stay behind? He knows that it was to avoid later guilt. So, is he really staying behind for himself? And, if that is true, then why should he feel that the guilt for leaving would have been any worse than the guilt for placing his own need for the laudanum over the Mexican's? He is sharing it, after all, isn't he?

Sanchez has started moaning now, and Asher's mind is forced out of the abstract and back into the concrete. He starts to raise the bottle to his lips, but then slowly lowers it. Something indefinable is gnawing at him. He will help Sanchez first, and then himself.

He moves off the saddle onto one knee and again lifts Sanchez's head gently and extends the bottle, and again the Mexican motions for Asher to go first. But this time Asher shakes his head, and so Sanchez takes his sip.

Asher now sits back onto his saddle and looks at the laudanum bottle in his hand, still uncorked. It looks as lovely to him as Beulah did on their wedding night. The deep ache is there in his back, as it always is, but Asher is not thinking about *that* pain. He is thinking about his need for the laudanum as a thing in and of itself. The pain in his back is bad, but he could delay a dose for *that*. But he does not truly think that he *can* delay it. Why is this?

Because he knows his desire for the laudanum is for another reason altogether, apart from the agony in his back. But try as he might, he cannot define that need. He cannot even determine if it is only in his mind, and its very murkiness in his thoughts troubles him greatly. The laudanum has taken on a life of its own.

Sanchez has drifted back off, or at least his eyes are shut, and he is resting peacefully. Asher looks at the bottle again, and it now seems nearer to half full than three-quarters. He knows that his sip will halve the original amount in the bottle. Four more doses for them. Four.

Now Asher begins his usual calculations. Suppose he could skip this dose and hold out for an hour. Then after a mutual dose in another hour after that, he could skip the one after *that*. This would give the old man two extra doses, two or three extra hours of relief.

Wishful thinking. Asher stares at the landscape, and the light of the mid-afternoon sun seems to him to be bathing it in a cold, amoral illumination. He needs the laudanum, and he needs it *now*. He raises it to his lips and again stops. He lowers it.

Just one hour. Surely, he can go without it for *one hour*. What is going to happen when he runs out, anyway? One hour. He can think about the beauty of the next sip for one hour, can't he? Instead of the self-loathing that would result from taking a sip *now*?

He puts the cork back in the bottle and re-wraps it in the rag.

And now he sits, rocking back and forth in his growing need, and his mind casts about for anything else to think on.

There *is* nothing else in the world to think about, except Sanchez.

He regards the old man now, and he begins to consider what he must be enduring. He thinks about the shock of what the bullet must have felt like, and he finds that he cannot imagine it. He considers what it must be like to know that you are about to die, and he finds that he cannot imagine it. He wonders how frightening it must be to be spending your last hours in a strange, unknown place with someone like himself, and he finds that he cannot imagine it. And then, from somewhere deep inside of him, he suddenly imagines all of it at once.

The realization comes to him that the old man isn't an emaciated dog, chained to a tree. He is a *man*, like himself, and suddenly he is looking at himself again the way the old man sees *him*. He imagines the old man seeing him doing all the right things, but he also imagines the old man knowing that these actions are not being done for the right reasons. He sees himself detached from any real compassion, and now he feels the deep anguish that this must be causing the dying man.

He sees himself as the wretch that he is, at his core, and for the second time in his life, he is grieved at what he has become.

How can this be? Was he not baptized in the shed blood of Christ Jesus? Was his soul not cleansed of all unrighteousness? Asher knows now that if his sin *was* washed away, he has let it all back in.

He sees himself now, with complete clarity, from within. He does not see himself as the affable, upright man that he wants the world to see. He knows that the things about himself that people regard as virtuous have been primarily the results of circumstance, and not design, or of conscious posturing for others, and not the inevitable fruit of a righteous man. He even realizes that helping the Mexican would be much easier if there was someone there to admire him for it.

His love for Beulah is the purest thing he knows, and even *that* is saturated with self.

Now he realizes that he is thinking of *doing* good instead of *being* good, and he instinctively understands that this is somehow backward.

Suddenly, a feeling comes to him: he is merely talking to himself. Baying at the moon. Where does all this self-righteousness come from?

But then it occurs to him to ask himself further: where did all this *doubt* just come from?

He brushes all that aside in his mind, and now he has one desire, even if it is partially self-serving. He wants to make the old man's passing as peaceful as he possibly can.

His mind comes back to the immediate, to his stark need for the laudanum, and to the old man lying in front of him. The part of himself that is detached from his need senses now the notion that he can, in some limited way, not make this *right*, but perhaps make it *easier*.

To keep his mind away from the laudanum, Asher decides to lay out his bedroll and get the firewood stacked so that when it gets dark, all he will need to do is set it alight. It is miserable work, but that seems better to him than miserable leisure.

At 4:45, when Sanchez comes back to consciousness, Asher is sitting on his saddle, ready with the laudanum. Asher takes his sip and then helps the old man. They both wait for the wonderful numbness.

To Asher's surprise, the old man does not drift away this time but seems more attentive. He is weaker now; he is not moving much, and when he does, it is sluggish movement, void of energy.

Asher wishes now that he could speak the old man's language. Such things do not come easily for him. The work of a Ranger does not specifically require it, and he has never before felt it necessary to learn it. Now he is becoming almost anguished at his inability to talk to the old man, as much for what he could *hear* as for what he could *say*.

They are quiet for a while, and then the old man startles Asher by saying softly, "*Necesito decir algo.*"

Asher shrugs gently and raises his hands. "I don't understand," he says, and then he remembers the stock phrase: "*No comprende.*"

The old man looks pensive for a moment, and Asher can see that he is trying to break through his laudanum fog to think of a way to get his point across. "*Por favor,*" he says, and then suddenly an idea crosses his face. He slowly pulls his bloody hands from beneath the bedroll and makes an odd gesture. The left hand is flat, and the right one has his thumb and first two fingers together. He takes his right hand and moves it across the palm-up surface of his left hand.

Asher parses the gesture, and suddenly he thinks he understands. "You want to write something down?" he asks.

The old man looks at him blankly, so Asher painfully moves off of his saddle and opens his left saddlebag and fumbles within. He finds a pencil in short order and holds it up to Sanchez, who smiles weakly and nods. But the only paper he has is a brittle, yellowed copy of the Laredo newspaper that has been in there for months, if not years. He looks quickly through the paper and finds some blank space in one of the quarter-page advertisements. He slides off his saddle and offers the pencil to Sanchez.

The old man shakes his head ruefully. "*Lo siento*," he says. "*No puedo leer ni escribir.*"

From this, Asher judges that the old man is saying that he is illiterate. He considers this for a moment and is grateful that the sip of laudanum has given him relief enough to think clearly. He takes the pencil in his right hand, and folds the newspaper enough to have surface support to write, and asks Sanchez, "Is this what you want?"

The old man smiles and starts to speak, and Asher takes the pencil and starts to write in the white space in the advertisement but finds that he needs his spectacles. He holds up his hand, and the old man stops speaking, and he quickly pulls them from his vest pocket, puts them on, and shuts his left eye because the spectacles have a cracked lens. Then he gets ready again and says, "Okay."

The Mexican's face suddenly turns very serious, and he says, with much formality, "*Permítanme comenzar diciendo que no puedo agradecerles lo suficiente.*"

This comes from Sanchez in that Hispanic way that has always seemed soft and lazy to Asher's ears. Asher is utterly and completely overwhelmed, and he makes no attempt to start writing this down. Instead, he smiles and looks sheepishly at Sanchez and shrugs. The Mexican smiles back, weakly.

"*Permítanme comenzar,*" Sanchez says quickly, and then stops.

Asher writes what he hears phonetically, slowly sounding it out to Sanchez as he writes. "Pear meeton may co main zar."

"*Permítanme comenzar*," Sanchez repeats, slower this time.

Reading again from the paper, Asher repeats exactly what he said the first time.

"*Permítanme comenzar*," Sanchez says one more time, even more slowly. Asher is missing something.

Asher reads it back slowly, trying to match Sanchez's pace.

At this, the old man regards Asher for a moment, then smiles again, and shrugs. "*Bueno*," he says.

"Bueno," Asher repeats, grateful for the old man's surrender.

The dance begins. The old man speaks, and Asher writes phonetically what he hears and repeats it back. Corrections are made, and gradually the old man begins to use phrases rather than sentences. Sometimes when Asher speaks back, the Mexican laughs a little and then repeats it, and Asher catches the difference and wonders exactly what he has just literally said, in Spanish. For the most part, though, it is a straightforward transaction: the Spanish, then the laborious phonetic transcription, followed by Asher's wooden repetition of the sounds that he has heard. Asher fills the original blank space around the advertisement, and then writes in the margins of the newspaper, using arrows and numbers to keep track of the direction of writing as he moves first from margin to margin, and then from page to page. He begins to worry about his ability to put all of this back together in any coherent way.

At one point, Asher finishes reading back what he has just transcribed, and when he looks back up expectantly at the Mexican, he sees that he has drifted into sleep. He pulls his pocket watch out and sees that it is coming up on 5:45, and he knows that the old man will not sleep long because they are nearing the end of the laudanum cycle.

He uses these few minutes to look at Sanchez, and he finds himself seeing something new. He appears *different* somehow, in a way that Asher cannot define. There is an odd nobility to him now, a spark of something in his expressions and mannerisms, a humanity that Asher did not see there at the beginning. Asher wonders what it is that has changed his perception of the old man.

At 6:15 the pain rouses Sanchez again, and he looks at Asher as though he is embarrassed to need more of the opiate. Asher lets him take his sip, and then he sits back on his saddle and resists the urge to take one himself. He missed one cycle and made it through. Surely, he can miss another one. There is less than half a bottle now, and the thought of what it will mean, for Sanchez, when it is gone, fills him with an apprehensive sorrow that overwhelms all other thoughts. He resolves to be stoic for the next hour and not to let Sanchez see either his pain or his need.

When Sanchez is again in the grip of the laudanum's relief, Asher picks up the paper and holds it and the pencil up for the old man to see. Sanchez smiles, but then looks a bit confused, so Asher repeats back the last phrase the Mexican had uttered before he drifted off.

"*Sí, eso es correcto,*" he says, and starts anew.

Asher can see now that the old man is fading. He is losing mental clarity, and his skin is taking on a gray pallor. Asher hopes fervently that the old man has enough time left to say everything he wants.

Finally, just before 7:00, the old man says, "*Eso es todo,*" and falls silent.

"Ay so ace toe doe," Asher repeats back.

"*Terminado,*" the old man says, and now Asher understands.

Asher holds the paper up to the old man. "Who?" he asks.

The old man considers this for a moment, and Asher cannot tell if he is trying to figure out what Asher is asking, or the answer to the question. After a moment, Sanchez says, "*Padre Valdez.*"

"Father Valdez," Asher says, and the old man nods, and closes his eyes.

At 7:30, just at sundown, Asher gives Sanchez and himself another sip of the laudanum. Asher's takes hold in the usual five minutes, but Sanchez continues to hurt, and Asher's very worst fears are beginning

to materialize. He gives Sanchez a second sip, and after a few minutes, the old man drifts away.

Asher looks at the bottle. There is an inch of the amber fluid left.

It is a clear night, and the stars are beginning to come into view, and Asher lights the fire and unrolls his bedroll. Then he sits back on his saddle, staring into the flickering flames, and slowly readies himself for the ramifications of a decision he has already made.

The remaining laudanum is for Sanchez.

He does not know if he will have the strength when the time comes for Sanchez's next dose. It is one thing to feel optimistic about it *now*, because he is currently enjoying the dose he just had. And he thinks that he will have the strength to skip the next dose, as he has been doing every other time. But what is going to happen to him after that?

He finds himself hoping that Sanchez will die soon, and he examines his heart to see if he wants that because it will ease the Mexican's suffering, or because there is a possibility that there might be some laudanum remaining in the bottle when it is all over. Asher is too tired to thrash through the difference, but he knows now that he has come to loathe the laudanum, once his dearest friend. He does not like the hold it has on him, and he does not like the thoughts that it is bringing to his mind.

Asher again returns his full attention to the old man. Sanchez's breathing is growing very shallow now, and Asher can sense that he is slipping away. He is suddenly struck by the notion that every time the old man's pain rouses him back into consciousness, there is every chance that his return to unconsciousness will be his final fade from the world. This thought incubates in Asher a sense of wonder, and now he is back in the old man's skin, looking at himself and the fire and the stars, and knowing that it is all going to recede. He wonders how the old man can bear the uncertainty of what that means. This realization propels Asher's mind into considering what he can say or do, if the old man comes back around, to help give him peace. Asher prays volitionally for wisdom in this matter.

The minutes pass. Asher is in a reverie, and the moon, waxing gibbous, rises in the eastern sky. It generates enough illumination to make visible even the far horizon, and it overpowers the light of the dimmer stars, flickering them out.

At 8:15 the old man suddenly cries out and becomes agitated and starts to sit up. He is in severe pain, and he is looking for any change that could bring relief. Asher moves over with the laudanum and brings it to Sanchez's lips, and he takes a sip, halving the small amount still in the bottle. Asher sits back, and he and the old man look at each other deeply while they wait for the pain to recede. Five minutes go by, and there is some relief, but not much, and Asher can see the panic begin to rise in the old man's face. They wait a few minutes more, and then Asher moves back over to him, wordlessly lifts his head, and gives him the last of the amber fluid.

The pain subsides now, but Sanchez begins trembling uncontrollably and Asher, without any hesitation, moves over and raises the old man and takes him in his arms, drawing the Mexican's bedroll up and around and over both of them. Sanchez burrows into Asher, and the shaking subsides.

The old man's breathing begins to level out, and Asher thinks he has dropped back out of consciousness. It surprises him, therefore, when Sanchez, whose face Asher can no longer see, says quietly, "*Como se llama?*"

"*No comprende,*" Asher says.

"*Me llamo Emilio Sanchez,*" the old man says, with more eloquence than Asher has ever heard in his entire life.

"*Asher. Me llamo Thomas Asher.*"

There is a pause for a moment, and then Sanchez says, "*Señor Asher. Gracias, mi amigo. Por todo.*" There is a further pause, and then the old man says, finally, "*Algo maravilloso se acerca.*"

After a while, the Mexican's breathing again becomes regular. Then, to Asher's sad and bittersweet relief, it begins to slow down, imperceptibly at first, but then noticeably. This goes on for some time, and Asher waits patiently and begins rocking the old man in his arms.

"Let go of it," Asher whispers to him. "You're almost there."

Asher will wonder later if the old man would have considered it disrespectful that Asher is unaware of the moment of actual release. There is no final convulsion and no death rattle. There is just the sudden realization that the shallow breathing has stopped and that decades of existence have come to an end. Asher is not at all startled to notice this and he continues to slowly rock the body back and forth. After a while, he very gently disengages, and as he lays the old man back on the bedroll, he kisses him on his cooling forehead.

Asher lies down by the fire while the night passes.

At six o'clock, despite the morning clouds, the reddish pre-dawn glow provides enough light to see. Asher rises to his feet and stands unsteadily, waiting for his legs to get their life back. His back is aching monstrously, and the need for laudanum is so great that he shuts his eyes and begins quietly to weep. But then he looks down at the still form of Emilio Sanchez and regains his composure.

It is all over now, and Asher's emotions are beginning to come back into alignment with his immediate situation. He has given no thought to what he will do now, and the prospect of the pain of having to pack everything up, including having to wrestle Sanchez's body onto the back of an animal, fills him with dread.

He must now consider whether his gesture with the shovel was merely to help Emilio Sanchez have peace, or if he had made a promise. He begins to walk painfully in the direction he had thrown the shovel.

He knows that if he buries Sanchez here, that will be the end of it. There will be no coming back to formally exhume the body. Moates will see to that, and Asher will let it happen because of the security this will bring to himself. He would stay on the payroll because Moates would need him to remain quiet. The other Rangers will go along with whatever Moates and Miller dictate. Sanchez will return to dust undisturbed, and his animals and gear will be quietly disposed of, and it will be as if he had never existed. There might be the odd query coming across the wire once in a while, but it would be safely ignored.

He knows that this is what Moates and Miller expect.

Asher finds the shovel about thirty feet from where he had thrown it, and he painfully picks it up and walks back to the smoldering fire and then stands quietly, gazing down again at Sanchez. The light is strong enough now that he can see that the old man actually seems dead, and not sleeping. Asher would be hard put to define exactly what the difference is, but it is there, and it is very stark. Asher wishes now that he could remember the old man's final words, to ask about them later.

He looks up at the sunrise, and it seems to him to be a symbol of renewal, and he remembers the relief on the old man's face when he threw the shovel, and he remembers that final 'thank-you,' and his heart decides for him that what he said to Sanchez was a promise, and not a bromide. He knows that he must try to do the right thing. He hopes that it won't be too costly, because of what it might mean for Beulah, but he knows that he must see this through. He looks down at Sanchez.

"This one thing," Asher says.

7

Hoisting the body of Emilio Sanchez onto the old man's pack mule is a nightmare for Asher.

His pain is so all-consuming that he finds himself taking the path of least resistance during the entire process of getting packed. He does not reload his own pack mule with the provisions on the ground; the supplies and the food, except for some jerky that he cuts out for later, remain on the ground where he had placed them the afternoon before. Even the shovel remains behind. It takes him ten minutes to get the sorrel saddled, and ten more to get Sanchez's saddle cinched firmly back in place. He considers just leaving it but decides that he wants everything of Sanchez's to go with them. If asked, he could not explain this.

After a moment's reflection, he decides to put Sanchez on the back of the pack mule, rather than on Sanchez's horse. There are two reasons for this: the mule is lower to the ground, which means less effort to get the body up onto it, and he wants the mule weighed down, to rob it of its energy and its natural tendency to be contentious.

Asher puts the saddle back on the pack mule and then spends fifteen painful minutes reloading all of the old man's possessions on the ground onto the Mexican's horse. When this effort is finished, he walks over to his own horse and rests his head against his saddle, waiting for the pain to subside a bit. He feels nauseous and has the shakes.

Asher does not know yet which direction he is going to go: he has the option of heading east to Falfurrias, or north to San Diego and a possible rendezvous with Miller. He does not have a firm idea of his exact position, and so he does not know which one is closer.

He will consider this as he packs up and decide as he departs.

Asher does not want to take Sanchez's body to wherever he is going without it being covered; the old man deserves more respect than that. It has been cold overnight, so rigor mortis is only just now beginning to set in. Asher knows that he needs to get the Mexican onto the pack mule before it begins in earnest.

Asher takes Sanchez's bedroll and splits it open and spreads it out, and then pushes the Mexican's body, with a great and painful effort, onto one side of it. He then rolls it, as tightly as he can, inside the blanket. It takes three and a half rolls to reach the other side of the blanket, so the old man ends up face down. No part of him is visible.

Asher stands up and is considering how to get the body onto the pack mule when he is struck by a notion that he has not considered. He has not, in any way, examined Sanchez's body, except for the cursory glance at his wound. Despite his intense physical discomfort, he finds himself curious about what any items on the body could tell him, especially whatever it was that he had been reaching for in his shirt pocket. He struggles to recall if any of the other Rangers had actually bothered to see what was there and can remember no such search. He cannot even remember any curiosity about it. Everyone had been too shocked to consider it. When he reflects on it, he cannot understand their collective lack of curiosity about a man whose life they have just ended. No one has followed through on why the old man was headed to San Diego.

Asher bends back down and laboriously unrolls the body, and it ends being back face-up. Then he moves the serape back and reaches into the old man's shirt pocket and retrieves a single yellow sheet of folded paper. Blood has seeped onto the left side of it. Asher unfolds it, almost reverentially.

It is a sender's copy of a telegram, initiated by a Father Roberto Valdez of Matamoros, in Mexico, from the Brownsville Western Union office to a Father Pedro Bard, in care of St. Francis de Paula Catholic Church in San Diego. The text of it says simply, "SENDING SOME-ONE FOR IT STOP MANY THANKS STOP."

So, the old man was headed to San Diego to get something for the priest in Matamoros. San Diego it is, then. Asher will head due north.

Asher refolds the paper and puts it into his own shirt pocket, and then examines the body again. There is nothing else on the old man, except for a belt which, now that Asher has noticed it, seems far larger and much nicer than would seem necessary to hold up a pair of tattered cotton trousers. Asher unfastens it in front, and before he has even finished pulling it off, he knows that it is a concealed money belt.

Folded neatly inside it, along its entire length, are forty American dollars, in greenbacks. This represents, to Asher, almost two weeks of wages. It must have seemed an almost unimaginable sum to an illiterate Mexican peasant. He concludes that this money was going to be used to pay for whatever Sanchez was going to San Diego to get.

Asher considers putting the belt in his own saddlebag, but he does not want there to be the slightest doubt about his integrity or his intentions, so he wraps it back around the old man's waist. Then he re-rolls the old man's body back into the blanket.

The final task is the hardest for him, by far: getting the old man's body onto the pack mule. He considers the logistics for a moment and decides that it is probably the fastest and best to just ignore his pain and try to lift it on himself. This he attempts, only to end up on his knees beside the mule, weeping in agony, with the body lying next to him on the ground. After regaining his composure, he thinks to take the lariat from his saddle and loop it around the rolled blanket, using the curve of the old man's feet for purchase. Then, he moves his horse to the other side of the pack mule, wraps the other end of the rope around the horn of his own saddle, and then slowly walks his horse forward, so the body is carefully dragged up onto the mule. This takes three attempts before it finally succeeds. He then ties the blanketed body onto the pack mule's saddle in such a way that it will not drift out of place.

It is 8:30 now, and he scans the campsite one final time, to make sure that he has not overlooked anything. Then he hauls himself painfully into his saddle, picks up the reins of the three animals, and sets out due north.

What can be said of the next twelve hours? Asher's pain is so depthless, and his obsession with the lack of laudanum so overwhelming, that it all becomes one long scream to him. He pushes on relentlessly, punishing the animals far beyond what he has ever done before because all he can think about is bringing this journey to an end. Asher knows that if he stops, he will get off the sorrel and lie down on the hard ground to ease his pain, and he is afraid that he would decide not to get up again, assuming that he even *could*. His nausea is unrelenting.

The ground is not especially difficult to move over, but it seems endless. There are no homesteads, no roads, nothing: just a vast, painful moving forward toward a taunting horizon.

The sun rises to its height for the day and begins its descent, and Asher loses all track of time and distance. He does not retrieve his pocket watch from his vest pocket because he knows that it will guarantee despair: it will either be earlier than he supposes, which will mean that he has farther to go, or it will be later, which means that he is running out of daylight. He rides as stoically as possible, head down, keeping his mind as far away from himself as he possibly can.

He continues northward through the eternal scrubland, fording the occasional dry or shallow creek bed, waiting for something to come into view that will give him some idea of his location. By midafternoon, he knows that he must be slowly converging on the railroad tracks that run north-east from Hebbronville to San Diego, and his spirits begin to rise a little.

Two hours later, he intersects the tracks and parallels them north-east toward San Diego, hoping that he is beyond Benavides, and he stays about twenty yards south of the elevated track-bed, where the land is easier for the animals.

Most of the previous two days had seen Miller and his men riding back and forth along the line that separates Duval County from Brooks County, looking for either riders or their tracks. It does not surprise any of them that they had not encountered either one. They ride into San Diego late in the afternoon on Friday. Miller has informed Burnett and Anspach that they will need to come with him to Laredo for a day or two until everything is sorted out.

The four of them proceed directly to the train depot, where they learn that the next train to Laredo is at 6:20.

Miller releases Anspach and Teeter for an hour to get something to eat but keeps Burnett with him, much to Burnett's chagrin. Miller goes into the depot and secures four tickets to Laredo, and a place on a stock car for four horses and a mule. He is relieved to find that Render Moates has already made the necessary financial arrangements.

Miller walks back out to the siding to rejoin Burnett, who is sitting in humiliated silence on one of the platform benches. "Let's get a bite to eat," he says. They go into the spartan café at one end of the depot and get a table and order a couple of sandwiches and a Sarsaparilla each. Miller himself wants a beer more than he cares to admit, but he doesn't want to inflame either Burnett's anger or his thirst.

While they are eating, the Duval County Sheriff walks into the diner with one of his men, scans the room, and walks over to Miller's table. He has obviously been informed that they are there. Without being asked, he and the deputy sit down.

Miller knows Amos Beauchamp by reputation, but they have never met. Duval County is Archibald Parr's County, top to bottom, and this man is his handpicked law dog. Miller does not know what Beauchamp wants, but he knows that he doesn't want to deal with him.

The four men perfunctorily introduce themselves.

"What brings you boys here?" Beauchamp asks.

"We had a report earlier in the week of an armed contingent of Mexican Nationals heading this way," Miller says. "We've been out trying to intercept them."

Beauchamp laughs out loud. "You boys still believe that 'San Diego Manifesto' bullshit?" he asks. Miller doesn't answer, and Beauchamp shakes his head with exaggerated incredulity. "There ain't nothing like that could happen in this county without us knowing it," he says and laughs again.

"You enjoying this?" Miller asks.

"You bet I am," Beauchamp answers. "When I see Texas' finest acting stupid, I know there's hope for the rest of us dumb peons."

From across the table, Burnett says, "Why don't you two shitkickers just move along? Maybe go shine Archie Parr's boots or something."

The mirth on Beauchamp's face evaporates instantly and he stands up so quickly his chair tips over. "You want to repeat that?" he asks.

Miller is relieved that Beauchamp's hand is nowhere near his gun, but he needs to defuse this situation immediately. "Shut up," he says angrily to Burnett, who looks down at his plate and says nothing further.

Burnett will never realize this, but he has just destroyed Render Moates' career as a Texas Ranger.

Beauchamp is still staring at Burnett. "I may have one more coming in," Miller says, trying to change the subject. "His name is Asher."

"Well," Beauchamp says, looking back to Miller, "we'll make him feel right at home."

At 6:00 all the men have reassembled, and the horses and pack mule are placed on a stock car, and the men file aboard the passenger car. The four men sit together, in two of the nicer seats that face each other. At 6:20, the train pulls out and begins the four-hour journey to Laredo. For the duration of the trip, Miller stares out the window at the darkness, while the other three sleep.

Just after ten o'clock, the train pulls into the depot in Laredo, where the men had headed out in the other direction sixty-five hours before. Moates is waiting for them, as impeccably dressed and formal as ever, shaking the hands of each of the men as they exit from their car. Miller notices that Burnett does not make eye contact with Moates. The animals are brought off the stock car and taken away to the livery. The men disperse to their homes or hotel, but Miller remains behind.

As soon as he and Moates are alone, Miller says, "Burnett got drunk and killed a civilian."

Miller watches Moates absorb the information, and he marvels at his unflappability as he considers it. There is no reaction at all, nothing: no pursed lips, no widened eyes, no anger. After a moment, he asks Miller two questions that startle him.

"What civilian, and where?"

"Mexican," Miller answers. "Middle of nowhere. Probably Duval County. We stopped him for questioning, and it just happened."

"Was he anybody?" Moates asks.

Miller consciously wonders if it is possible for Moates to drag him any lower. "No," he says, almost against his will.

"And this man is dead?"

"He is by now," Miller says. "Asher stayed with him."

Now, to Miller's complete surprise, Moates shrugs and says, "Well, there's nothing we can do about this tonight. Be at my office at 9:00 in the morning, and we'll figure out where to go from here."

So Miller goes home, and he is so utterly weary that he gives Leona only the most general details of his time away. He does not mention Sanchez at all. Not yet. But Leona Miller knows her husband's rhythms: the way he carries himself, the way he sleeps, and the way he speaks. This night, none of them are quite right.

Moates telephones him at home at 5:30 the next morning and informs him that he needs to see him at 6:00, instead of 9:00. Thirty minutes later, Miller walks into Moates' office. He is surprised to find Teeter there, sitting across the desk. Miller does not sit.

"Lyle has given me an account of what happened," Moates says.

Miller is furious with Teeter but reckons that he cannot let Moates see that. He looks at the young man, who is inwardly delirious with happiness because Moates has just called him by his first name.

Miller turns to Moates and is about to speak when Moates cuts him off. He is standing up, and visibly angry. "I received a telegram sent last night waiting for me early this morning from Beauchamp, the sheriff over in Duval County. Thorough-going ass." Moates sits down. "Asher showed up in San Diego last night with the greaser's body. Asher told Beauchamp that he wants to take it straight back to Mexico."

Now Miller sits down. He feels a sense of dread coming over him.

"Lyle," Moates says to Teeter, "thank you so much for your help here. For *all* your help. I need time with Sergeant Miller now."

Miller vaguely wonders what Moates means by '*all* your help.'

Teeter leaves, and Moates turns to Miller. "Do you realize that this puts me in Archie Parr's pocket? What were you thinking? Why in God's name did you leave the Mexican with *Asher*?"

"As opposed to what?" Miller asks. "Anyway, Asher volunteered." He pauses, then asks, "What are you going to do?"

"Well, we can't have Asher going to Mexico with a dead national and no formal explanation," Moates says. "I am going to politely ask Beauchamp to send the body here. An inquest can keep a lid on things."

"How will that help?" Miller is genuinely puzzled.

"Teeter has explained to me that the Mexican made a gesture that could be considered threatening."

"No," Miller says. "Burnett was drunk and shot him by accident."

"Miller," Moates says, "you need to get your damned head clear."

Asher rides into San Diego an hour after sundown on Friday night with the horse and the two pack mules in tow. He is weary beyond measure, his back has collapsed, and the withdrawal from the laudanum remains all-consuming. He stops a pedestrian under a streetlamp at an intersection and, looking down from his saddle, asks for directions to the Sheriff's office. He is in such obvious distress that the man gives him what he needs without asking about the body draped over the pack mule.

Ten minutes later, Asher walks through the door of the Duval County Sheriff's office. There is a single deputy on duty, sitting at a desk, reading the newspaper. The man sees Asher's badge just under his open, bloodied coat, and says, "You must be Asher."

"I need to see the sheriff," Asher says.

The deputy nods and reaches for the telephone. Ten minutes later, a large, burly man comes in briskly through the front door.

"Amos Beauchamp," he says, extending a hand. "Miller and the other men came in this afternoon, and they all went back to Laredo on the 6:20. Caused quite a commotion. Miller said you might be coming in later." They shake hands.

Beauchamp motions to the front door. "He didn't say anything about a corpse."

"Well, he should have," Asher says.

"Well, he didn't," Beauchamp says, in a tone that makes it clear that he doesn't appreciate the surprise.

"His name was Sanchez," Asher says. "He was a Mexican national. He was shot by accident yesterday morning. Died during the night. Twenty-five, maybe thirty miles south of here. Been riding all day."

"Who shot him?" Beauchamp asks.

Asher evades the question. "We stopped him yesterday morning. Things just went bad. Did Miller explain to you what we been doing?"

"Yep," Beauchamp says. "Ridiculous waste of time. Just absurd." He moves away from Asher and walks to the barred windows overlooking the street outside, and gazes at the animals tethered in front. Finally, he turns to Asher. "You work for Render Moates, am I right?"

"I work for the State of Texas," Asher replies. "I *report* to Render Moates."

"I'd make that distinction, too, if I had to work for him," Beauchamp says. "I guess I need to take formal possession of the body."

"And his horse and pack mule," Asher says.

Beauchamp nods and looks over at the deputy at the desk, who has been listening intently. "Get that man's body over to Selkirk's," he says. "Tell him I will get with him in the morning. Then take *all* these animals to the livery stable." Beauchamp has noted Asher's weakened state. The deputy gets up and leaves through the front door.

Beauchamp turns back to Asher. "I got dinner guests," he explains. "Can we take this up in the morning? You look like you could use a good night's sleep. There is a hotel right across the street. The next train back to Laredo is at 11:15 tomorrow morning."

"I ain't going to Laredo," Asher says. "As soon as I can get the body, I am taking him home, to Brownsville."

"Brownsville? I thought you said he was Mexican."

"Matamoros," Asher says. Matamoros is directly across the Rio Grande from Brownsville.

"Well, we'll discuss that in the morning," Beauchamp says. "Why don't you go get some sleep? And a bath, while you're at it."

Asher half-walks and half-staggers his way across the street and checks into the hotel. He is indifferent to the type of room he is given, or the cost, or the availability of a bath. When he gets up to his room, he simply removes his boots and lies down on the bed. Within a few minutes, he surrenders the bed for the relative comfort of the hard floor on his back, but this does not alleviate his pain enough for consistent sleep. He spends a terrible night, alternately bemoaning his pain, and his need for some laudanum.

At 8:30 the following morning, he is sitting at a table in a café down the street from the hotel, staring at a cup of coffee, when Beauchamp walks in and sits down across from him.

"You okay?" he asks, noting Asher's demeanor and pallor.

"Been better," Asher says.

"I can't release the body to you," Beauchamp announces abruptly.

"Why?" Asher knows the answer but asks, anyway.

"Moates got back to me a little while ago. I telegraphed him last night. He says there is going to be an inquest in Laredo, and the body needs to be shipped there. It is going out on the 11:15."

Asher shakes his head in a gentle, controlled frustration. "Why would they do an inquest in Webb County?" he asks. "The old man was killed right here in Duval County."

Beauchamp shrugs. "Maybe he was," he says, "and maybe he wasn't. From what you explained, he could have met his maker in Brooks County, or even Jim Hogg."

"It was Duval County," Asher says. "I'll testify to that fact."

"Not here you won't," Beauchamp says matter-of-factly. "Anyway, it's moot. Moates maintains that this is a state matter."

Asher can now see what Moates is doing, and the anger starts to rise in him.

"Moates says that this man was killed in the line of duty, probably with some justification," Beauchamp continues. "He says that the old man was reaching for a weapon when he was shot."

"No," Asher says. "He was reaching for *this*." Asher retrieves from his pocket the folded telegram.

"Doesn't matter," Beauchamp says, not even glancing at the paper, "if it even *looked* like he might have been reaching for a gun."

Asher leans back in his chair, and Beauchamp watches his latent anger evolve into a deep sadness. Beauchamp isn't unsympathetic. He essentially works for Archibald Parr, and he is experienced in the ways that power can be manipulated. He is inclined to let such things play out on their own. He lives with himself by imagining that he picks his battles very carefully. Although he has never actually picked one.

Anyway, all of this is of no consequence. Parr runs Duval County, and Parr wants Moates in his debt, and what Archie wants, Archie gets.

Asher considers his options and resolves to go west with the body, instead of south.

"What about his horse and pack mule?" Asher asks.

"They are going on the train with him. Yours, too, if you're going back on the same train."

"Is the old man being embalmed?" Asher asks.

"Can't," Beauchamp replies. "He's going back for an inquest. That may mean an autopsy."

"Is he in a coffin, or are you just shipping him back wrapped up like I brung him in?"

Instead of taking umbrage, Beauchamp shrugs off Asher's tone.

"Railroad won't take him like that. Moates said to put him in the cheapest pine box they got. He's footing the bill for all of it. We're leaving him wrapped up, though. I haven't even looked at him. That old boy is going to commence to go ripe."

Beauchamp wants to conclude this conversation, so he stands and says, "Good luck, Asher."

Asher thinks of the telegram in his hand and asks, "Can you tell me how to find St. Francis *something* Catholic Church?"

"St. Francis de Paula," Beauchamp says. "Victoria Street." An odd expression comes to his face. "Why are you asking?"

"See a priest," Asher says.

Moments later, Asher is standing in front of a moderately-sized Catholic church sitting at the intersection of Victoria and Church streets. He walks up the half-dozen steps to the level of the sanctuary and attempts to open the large wooden door. It is locked. He steps back and walks back down the steps and around to the back of the church.

He finds a priest there, cassocked and collared, whitewashing a small, rectangular outbuilding with a large brush. The priest sees him and motions a hello but continues with the brush until he finishes an exterior wall. Then he lays it down and walks over to Asher, hand extended. Asher now notices that the priest is older than his spryness at first glance led him to believe.

"Father Pedro Bard," he says, as he warmly shakes Asher's hand. "To whom do I have the honor?" An accent is noticeable but, curiously, it does not sound Spanish.

"My name is Asher." He opens his coat so that the priest can see his badge. "Do you have a few minutes?"

"Of course," the priest says and motions to the back door of the church. "How does a cup of hot tea sound?"

Ten minutes later, Asher is sitting in Father Bard's austere office, with a hot mug in his hands. The priest is holding the folded telegram.

"What was his name, again?" Father Bard asks.

"Emilio Sanchez."

"Well," the priest says, shaking his head, "I know a lot of Sanchezes, but no Emilio." He looks at Asher quizzically, raises the paper in his hand and says, "I received this telegram from the priest at the San Martin Cathedral in Matamoros a month or so ago. It involves an item that our church is giving to theirs."

"Which would be what?" Asher asks.

The priest stands. "I'll show you."

They walk out of the office through a door to the interior, into a large sanctuary rich with statuary and candles. The odor of incense is thick. They pass through that and enter a small side-chapel that seats perhaps sixty people. The silence, coupled with the overhead sun streaming in shallowly from the stained-glass windows, strikes Asher as somehow somber. They walk over to the small altar, and Father Bard says, almost whispering, "It's this." He is pointing to a large crucifix on the back wall, behind the altar.

It is a crucifix far too large for the wall. It is not mounted to the wall, but leans against it, at a tilt. The base of the crucifix is over three feet from the wall, halfway to the back of the small altar.

It is quite beautiful, made of a dark, lacquered hardwood. The statue of Christ, mounted to the wood in some way that is not obvious, is extremely detailed, in that distinctly Catholic way: small rivulets of blood have been painted on the hands and feet and forehead, and the face of Christ, looking up to heaven, is contorted with agony.

"This showed up quite unexpectedly, a year ago," the priest says, in a low voice. "They built a new Cathedral in Corpus Christi, and most of the old liturgical instruments and statuary in the old one were distributed to all the churches in the diocese. As you can see, this is just far too big for this small sanctuary."

"How tall is it?" Asher asks.

"Fourteen feet, top to bottom."

Asher is having trouble putting everything together in his mind. "You're telling me that Sanchez was going to haul this cross across the desert with a *pack mule*?"

"It's a crucifix," the priest says.

"Yes, a crucifix," Asher says.

The priest shrugs. "I have no idea. All I am telling you is that we had this crucifix available, and the Church in Matamoros wanted it."

Asher stands for a moment, trying to make sense of it, and can't. He looks at the priest and shakes his head, and shrugs, baffled.

They walk back into the priest's office and sit down. Their tea is cold, so the priest empties the mugs into a basin and pours more.

"The arrangement I made with Father Valdez was for them to send someone from their parish to come for it. They would pack it up and make their own arrangements to accompany it back to Brownsville. We simply cannot afford the freight on it. It mystifies me that Father Valdez would send someone to take it overland by horseback."

They are quiet for a time, and then Asher asks, "How did you make the connection with the church in Matamoros?" Asher asks this question as much to stall for time as to satisfy curiosity. He is very frustrated because he has no sense of what he should do now.

"I taught Father Valdez when he was at the orphanage up in San Antonio, about twenty years ago," Father Bard replies. "We have kept up a correspondence through the years."

"Á Mexican priest went to school here in Texas?"

"He is not really Mexican, although he looks it to some degree. His Spanish is fluent, though. He is a wonderful priest."

"If he ain't Mexican, what is he, then?"

"Well, he's American by birth. Interesting story. He was born in Arizona. His mother was a San Carlos Apache who died giving birth to him. His father was a Negro soldier who was killed before he was born."

"How did he end up being a priest?" Asher asks.

"The man who killed his father was at least part Mexican. That was the man that raised him. I don't know the details of that, but I imagine that it is fascinating. When he was eight years old, the old man became deathly ill and put him in the Catholic Orphanage in Tucson. I suspect that Roberto felt his vocation early, there. He certainly had it when I first met him, when he was fourteen. When that orphanage closed its doors, he was sent to the one in San Antonio."

"Why is he in Mexico?" Asher asks.

"Because he feels more Mexican than Anglo," Father Bard says. "He has more than one heritage to choose from." The priest pauses, then says, "You know, it takes a lot of courage to be a priest on that side of the river. He's probably safe, for now, even though Matamoros is occupied by the rebels. But both sides are beginning to kill priests in the interior of the country."

Asher has heard accounts of this, of the wholesale butchery going on down there, and nods. There is another silence, longer now. Asher is utterly unsure of what to say or do now.

"Are you yourself a Mexican?" Asher asks. "Your accent don't seem Spanish."

"French," the priest says.

"You said your name was Pedro," Asher says.

"Actually, it's Jean-Paul." He offers no additional detail.

There is a silence, and then the priest asks, "So you say Sanchez was killed, coming here?"

"It was an accident," Asher says. "I was thinking that he might have been coming home here, from there, or something." Asher does not wish to be evasive, and he is growing frustrated with the guilt he feels for his vagueness. But he feels the need to remain cautious.

"No," the priest says. "I wish I could provide more help."

"So do I," Asher says.

Another silence is beginning, so Asher surrenders his search for direction and stands up, reaches for his hat and coat, and goes to the back door. It is 10:15, and he has a train to catch.

He turns to the priest. "Thank you for your time," he says. "I don't know what to tell you about the cross."

The priest gently corrects him. "The crucifix."

"Yes, the crucifix," Asher says.

Asher verifies that all four animals are on a stock car and that the old man's plain pine box is on a freight car before he settles into a seat on one of the passenger cars. It pulls out of the San Diego depot at 11:15 on Saturday morning, headed west, to Laredo.

For a time, he watches the afternoon scenery go by, and he thinks. The face of Emilio Sanchez comes to mind, and for the first time since knowing what Sanchez was doing, he has time to reflect.

It will probably never be clear what Sanchez hoped to accomplish with the crucifix and the pack mule; it would simply never have worked. Perhaps if he meets with Father Valdez, there will be some sort of explanation. The time with Sanchez remains a vast mystery to him. He has bits and pieces of something in his mind, but he cannot put them all together in any coherent way.

Asher gradually fades into sleep, and a dream comes to him, and he is aware for its duration that he is *in* the dream. He is sitting on the train, exactly as he had been when awake, and he is looking at the facing seat across from him, and Emilio Sanchez is sitting there. This is not the worn and battered and dying Emilio Sanchez of the last three days, whose body now rests in the cheap coffin in the freight car. This is a finished and complete and beautiful Emilio Sanchez, dressed in immaculate white trousers and shirt, barefoot, and he is staring at Asher with a smile that contains the light of all the stars in the firmament.

The old man (although he is not old in this dream, and not young) says, in perfect English (or is it English?), "Something wonderful is coming." His lovely brown eyes are moist with joy.

And then Asher awakens so quickly and seamlessly that it seems as though he has only blinked. The seat across from him is empty.

At 3:45 they make the approach into Laredo. Asher stands and steadies himself as the train begins to slow. He moves to the front of the car and waits as the train comes to a stop. When he steps off the car onto the platform, he recognizes four men among the crowd, obviously waiting for his arrival: Moates and Miller, a man from the livery stable, and Farrell, from a local mortuary. The two Rangers walk up to him, but neither of them speaks to him or offers him a hand to shake. Asher reciprocates their aloofness. The tension hangs thickly in the air, like the odor of incense in the sanctuary at Father Bard's church.

They stand wordlessly and watch the liveryman get the four animals from the stock car. He has brought a livery wagon to tether them to, and he throws the four saddles into it and departs. Farrell directs some depot laborers to get the coffin off the freight car, and this goes onto the bed of another wagon, and Farrell takes it away.

The depot is finally quiet again, and now Moates turns to Asher.

"God damn you to hell," he says.

Asher looks over at Miller, who does not return his gaze. The look on Miller's face is one of badly-concealed embarrassment.

Asher turns and walks away. Moates says, behind him, "You bastard, don't you walk away from me." It takes all the self-discipline that Asher possesses to not look back.

"Asher!" Moates yells, and now those few other people still on the depot platform glance up. Asher cannot see that Moates has begun to walk down the steps after him, his face becoming purpled with anger. Miller puts his arm on Moates' elbow.

"Captain," he says quietly. "You can't do this here."

Moates jerks his arm away, but he *does* stop, staring at Asher's retreating form. He looks back at Miller, and then around him at the other people on the depot platform, and he regains his composure. He stares back after Asher again. "Son of a bitch," he says.

Asher walks the five blocks to the Sirocco Hotel, enters the lobby, and then regards with dread the bottom of the grand staircase. His back aches something fierce, and the six flights, as they always do, are going to take him from bad to worse. Since the accident, he arranges his days so that he only has to do it once.

He wants to make sure before he goes up that Beulah is there because he needs her and does not want to wait. He therefore walks back outside and goes to the alley on the right side of the building and walks down the wagon-wide way. As part of their rent, he and Beulah have access to a small room off the alley that Beulah uses to generate a little extra money. There is a small, hand-painted sign sticking out from the wall over the single door: "*Beulah Asher. Seamstress.*"

Beulah is there, hand-sewing a pair of trousers under the light of a single electric bulb. She looks up when he enters, and he is pleased to see the joy come to her face. She stands and moves to him and puts her arms around his waist and her head against his chest.

"I have been so worried," she says. "I saw this morning that the rest of you were back. When I asked Moates, he said you were delayed."

"He didn't tell you when I was coming in?" Asher asks.

"No," Beulah says. "Did he know?"

"He knew. He just didn't want you at the depot."

"What's happened?" Beulah asks.

"Beulah, I am hurting something fierce. I ain't had any laudanum for two days, and I need a bath and some decent sleep."

"Two days?" She thinks she has misheard what he said.

"Please," Asher says. "Can we just go upstairs?"

She turns off the light and shuts the door, and together they go inside and trudge slowly up to the sixth floor. This takes ten minutes.

Asher settles into a chair at the table, and Beulah pulls from the dresser an unopened bottle of laudanum. She walks over and places it on the table in front of him, next to his Bible and her *Middlemarch*.

Then she moves to the door. "I am going to go and draw you a hot bath," she says and goes back down the hallway.

She returns fifteen minutes later and is shocked to see that the bottle is still unopened. She looks at him questioningly, and he says quietly, "Let's see if I can put it off a little while."

They move down the dim hallway to the bath, and she removes his clothes for him, starting with his boots, as he sits painfully on the edge of the tub. She can smell the terrible week on him. When he is naked, she helps him into a bath with water so hot it causes him to flinch. But he slowly settles into it, and after a moment it begins to take hold. He sees the sudsy water begin to darken around him.

Beulah sits on the edge of the tub and rubs his back and shoulders gently with her hand and a bar of soap. He closes his eyes and would allow himself to drift away, but he knows that he will have to wake back up in a few minutes, as the water cools.

"Beulah," he says finally, "things went bad."

"How?"

"A man got killed who shouldn't have. It wasn't me that done it, but I stayed with him until he died. I don't know what this all means. They want it to go away."

She can hear the utter fatigue in his voice, almost despair, so she decides to wait for details, and to tell him of Leona Miller's visit later. To steer him away from his thoughts she says, "Want more hot water?"

He looks down and sees that the water is almost black. He remembers, for just an instant, the emotion of his baptism. On impulse, he slides his buttocks painfully forward and lowers his head beneath the water, and when he surfaces Beulah washes his hair with the soap.

Eventually, she helps him stand, and then dries him off, and then supports him, still naked, as they move back down the hallway to their room. He avoids their bed and lies down on the floor and is asleep within a few moments. He will never know it, but she sits there half the night, watching over him and loving him so much it hurts.

The following morning, when Asher wakes for good, Beulah helps him into a sitting position, as she always does. She sees that this hurts him very much, as it always does, and she sees him look for the laudanum bottle, as he always does. It is lying, still unopened, on the table. Then she sees him look away. What she does *not* see at any time during that day is Asher make any move toward it. She knows what he is enduring and is prouder of him than she has ever been.

At length, she helps him climb into a clean suit, and he glances at the time as he slides his watch into his vest pocket. It is 7:45 on Sunday morning.

"Beulah, I don't think I can make it to church this morning."

She doesn't press him. "Why don't we go down to the café for breakfast, and then see how you feel?"

"It ain't a question of how I *feel*," Asher says. "There's just things I need to do."

Beulah nods quietly, and the fact that she asks no questions paradoxically causes Asher to remember that she doesn't know much of what has happened. So, he tells her, in some detail, of the last four days, including his visit with the priest in San Diego the previous morning. When he finishes, she asks him, "What does Moates want you to do?"

"Whatever it takes to make this go away," he says. He looks at her, and she sees the concern in his eyes. "Beulah, I don't want to take the Rangers through the mud. God, I been with them half my life. But I am taking this man back to his people."

"I understand," she says.

"I just need you to understand that if I wanted to, I could use this to stay on the payroll," he says. "I could squeeze them real hard."

She says nothing, and her face betrays no concern.

"I just ain't inclined to do that," Asher says. "Something happened out there between me and that old man. I am taking him home."

She nods, and leans over and kisses his forehead, and stands up.

"I am hungry," she says.

At 8:30, they are sitting in the hotel dining room, eating the first hearty meal Asher has had in almost a week, when the minister of Moates' church, the Very Reverend Roscoe Jacobs of the Second Presbyterian Church of Laredo, Texas, comes in and walks to their table.

"May I join you?" he asks.

"Not if Render Moates sent you here, you can't," Asher says. Beulah is embarrassed by his palpable lack of respect, but she doesn't know Moates or understand the ways that he can come at you sideways.

Jacobs purses his lips and looks at Asher directly and says, "Well, he *did*, in fact, ask me to have a word with you." He sits down anyway. "Captain Moates tells me that you are a man of deep faith. He has explained to me what has happened, and I think you are to be commended for the ministry you performed for that unfortunate man."

"Get to the point," Asher says.

"I am supposed to convey to you how delicately something like this has to be handled. There are, how did he phrase it?, *nuances*."

"Consider it conveyed," Asher says.

"Mister Asher," Jacobs says, "I am in the middle here. Having said all this, I also want to say to you that you must do the righteous thing, whatever that is." He gets back to his feet. "The very effrontery of that man. Well, I can now tell Captain Moates, in all honesty, that I talked to you about this. He will ask me how you responded, and I will tell him that you had no response." He smiles. "My duty here is done, and the presbyters will be satisfied." And with that, the Very Reverend Roscoe Jacobs of the Second Presbyterian Church of Laredo, Texas walks out the door of the dining room without looking back.

"He seems like a good man," Beulah says. She is gently chiding Asher for his directness with Jacobs.

"Yes, and no," he replies. "He wants to do the right thing, as long as it don't cost him." But he considers these words almost immediately and feels some shame for his obvious hypocrisy.

"All of us do, I guess," he says.

After breakfast, they walk to the door of the hotel, and Beulah asks, "What are you going to do now?"

Asher pulls his watch from his vest pocket. It is 9:00. Around the town, they begin to hear church bells calling people to early services.

"I am going to Farrell's," he says. "I need to make arrangements about embalming the body."

"What about them doing an autopsy?" Beulah asks.

Asher has no answer. "I don't know. I just need to make sure that he's being treated with respect. I don't trust Moates. I don't know what he's capable of doing to make this go his way."

"Well," Beulah says. "I am going to go ahead on to church."

Asher walks through the center of town down Salinas Avenue, and turns right on Farragut Street, and walks three blocks to Farrell's Funeral Home. It is a standard two-story affair, a mansion really, in a formerly upscale part of town that is changing from Residential to Commercial. Asher walks up the steps onto a large porch and tries the front door. To his surprise, it opens.

He enters a beautifully appointed foyer, richly carpeted and exquisitely furnished. A bell over the door has rung, and after a moment Ernest Farrell steps into the foyer from an office to the right. They introduce themselves as they shake hands.

Asher gets right to the point. "I am here to see Emilio Sanchez."

"I remember you from the depot yesterday," Farrell says. "You brought him to Laredo."

"Can I see him?"

Farrell hesitates. "I have been instructed by Captain Moates not to let anybody go near him. He says that there is a possible inquest and that the body has to be protected."

Asher stares at Farrell impassively, and after a moment Farrell says, "I don't know what to tell you."

Asher can push this, but he is beginning to realize that seeing the old man is not actually why he is here.

"I need to ask you about embalming," he says.

"Moates says no embalming," Farrell says. "I got him on ice."

"I understand that," Asher says. "But what if you get word from Moates that it is okay, and that the body is to be released? How much time would that take?"

"To embalm him? I'd need at least a day."

"Suppose you got word this afternoon, or this evening?" Asher asks. "Could you have him ready by 5:00 tomorrow morning?"

"Can't be done," Farrell says. "I'd need more time. And anyway,

Moates ain't indicated that this is even a possibility."

"How much do you charge for embalming?" Asher asks.

"Twenty dollars for a basic job, but that ain't the issue."

"Suppose I paid you thirty dollars?"

Farrell shakes his head.

"And bought a nice coffin," Asher says.

Now Farrell hesitates. The possibility that this job might actually be lucrative is one that he has not even remotely considered.

Asher is making this up as he goes along. A notion has come into his mind, and he is now beginning to see it as something more than wishful thinking. He is not a forceful man, but he knows that to make this idea happen, he will have to push it, aggressively.

"Well?" Asher asks.

"I'd need to know by 6:00 tonight."

"I'll be back," Asher says.

9

Once Asher has exited Farrell's and is standing on the porch by the front door, he stops and tries to sort out the array of thoughts that seem to be coming at him from all sides. While talking inside, he had been struck with a notion that at first seemed unthinkable, but which is rapidly gaining purchase in his mind. It is an amorphous thing, and he needs to think through a way to break it down into specific actions.

His general fear is that if he doesn't act now, if he doesn't initiate some specific momentum toward making things right, toward seeing this thing through, that everything will grind down from inertia. He knows himself, and he knows that he is perfectly capable of waking up morning after morning in the weeks and months to come and feeling less inclined to act with each passing day.

This was the way that the laudanum had taken him over. A saddle cinch had broken, he had gone down, and his back would never be the same. Then, after months of deep pain, the doctor had him try the laudanum, and he had known, a month into enjoying the relief that it afforded him, that something was going amiss. He had considered the possibility that he was, in some vague way, robbing Peter to pay Paul. But each day that passed took from him incrementally any thought of dealing with it, and he realized one afternoon, standing by the sorrel and preparing to hoist himself up into the saddle, that the laudanum owned him. At that instant, he surrendered to it unconditionally.

A couple drives by in a dark blue Model T, and the driver tips his Sunday best hat to Asher as they pass him. He pulls his watch from his vest and sees that it is straight-up 10:00. At the same moment, church bells sound from somewhere in the distance.

Asher walks up Farragut Street back to the intersection of Salinas and pauses, unsure of what direction to take from there. The sound of an organ drifts by and then fades. Everything seems deathly still.

A drug emporium is there, where he has always procured his laudanum, and Asher suddenly thinks of the telephone on the back wall next to the apothecary, and his next action instantly occurs to him. He crosses the street and enters. The store is quite large, and he moves down the central aisle to the back wall. The telephone is there, and a woman is using it. He moves to the drug counter, where a young clerk is regarding him with mild interest, and says, "I need to make a call."

"A local call will be a nickel," the clerk says.

Asher pays him and when he turns the woman is gone. He walks over and lifts the earpiece and turns the crank. A few seconds elapse, and then a woman's voice says, "May I help you?"

"Render Moates, please."

There is a slight pause, and the woman says, "Do you want his home or his office?"

Asher guesses. "Home."

"One moment," the woman says, and then a rhythmic electrical sequence starts while Asher readies himself.

Fifteen seconds pass and Asher is about to hang up when there is a click, and another woman's voice says, "Moates residence." This will be Moates' wife, a pensive, reserved woman whom Asher has met several times in passing. He cannot recall her first name.

"Is the Captain in?" Asher asks.

"May I ask who is calling?" she says.

"Asher," he says. He leaves it at that.

"Yes, Mr. Asher," she says, after the briefest of pauses. "One moment." Then a curious thing happens. There is no sound of the earpiece being put down, no interruption of any sort, and she speaks again, almost immediately.

"Mr. Asher, before I get him, there is something I would like to say to you." Her voice has lowered.

"Yes?"

"Listen," she says, barely above a whisper, "whatever is going on here, don't give in to him. Do you understand me? Stand up to him."

He is quiet for a moment, with no idea about how to respond to this. Finally, he says, "Thank you."

"One moment," she says again, and now he hears the sound of the telephone earpiece being put down on a table.

After a moment, Moates' voice says suddenly, "Thomas. What a nice surprise." This startles Asher for a moment, and then he realizes that Moates' wife must be standing right there beside him.

"1:00. Your office," Asher says and hangs up.

He does not feel that he has committed himself by this action. He knows that he does not have to be there at 1:00 if he changes his mind. He knows that his employment by the State of Texas has probably come to an end and he enjoys, in an odd way, the freedom that affords him.

For the last hour, he has been so lost in thought that the pain in his back has been subdued, but now it is beginning to come back to the surface again. On his way out of the store, he purchases a bottle of aspirin, which would have been a laughable action just a week ago, and he takes four of them, downing them with water from the fountain by the door. Then he is back out on the street, at the intersection.

He knows now what he must do, and he continues on Farragut Street, in the direction he has been going, for two blocks, and then turns right on Santa Isabel. Another five blocks and he is at the train depot.

He goes inside and walks up to the ticket window. Aside from staff, there is not another person inside the building at all. He says to the agent, an attentive young man with a genuine smile, "I need to get some rate information and schedules."

"One moment, sir." The young man turns and moves out of sight, and after a moment a door opens ten feet down the wall, and an older man leans out and says, "Come on in."

And now they are sitting at the man's desk, and he has pulled a thick binder from a side-drawer. "Go ahead," he says.

"First, round-trip ticket, to Brownsville," Asher says.

The man does not even need to consult his book. "$6.40."

"Is the 5:15 the first one out of here in the morning?" Asher asks.

"Sure is," the agent says. "Nine stops, fifteen minutes each between here and Robstown. That part of the trip takes about eight hours. Then you transfer to a southbound train on the St. Louis line, destination Brownsville. That pulls out at 5:40 tomorrow afternoon, direct to Brownsville. You get in about 1:00 in the morning. So you'll have about a two-to-three-hour layover in Robstown."

"One of those stops is San Diego?" Asher asks.

The man nods. "Should pull through about 11:00 in the morning."

"I'll be taking one horse and one mule with me, both one way," Asher says.

"Two equines," the old man says, looking at the rate book. "$5.70."

Asher is keeping track. $12.10. "A coffin," Asher says.

The old man looks up. "Occupied?" he asks.

"Yes."

Back to the rate book. "$8.35." He looks back up. "One way."

$20.45. Asher is already rehearsing his discussion with Beulah. "These things will be transferred south automatically in Robstown?"

"Should be. No guarantees, though."

"One last thing," Asher says. "I will be having an item loaded onto the train in San Diego, also going on to Brownsville. If it is ready to load when my train pulls in, can it be loaded then?"

"Up to the station master," the old man says. "How big is it?"

"I don't know," Asher says. He does not want to describe it.

"That will be between you and the station master in San Diego," the old man says.

At 1:00 straight up, Asher arrives at the District Office. He wants to pause for a moment, to prepare himself, but he doesn't know if he is being observed from the inside, so he goes directly in. He does not want Moates to see his fear. He crosses the foyer and goes through the open door into Moates' office.

Moates is sitting behind his desk, and the room is full of men. Miller is there, and Anspach and Teeter. Burnett is there, a bit soberer now, but still bleary. Even Hardesty is there.

"Well, isn't *this* nice?" Asher says. "A Come to Jesus meeting."

A few of the men laugh softly, but then stop, because Moates doesn't laugh.

The men are milled about the room, sitting in the large leather chairs, or leaning against the pool table, or the nearest bare wall. There is a single chair in the middle of everyone, directly opposite Moates' desk, that sits empty. An interrogation, then. Moates motions to it.

"Sit down," he says.

"No," Asher says. "This won't take that long."

Moates flushes, because he is being challenged, for the first time in his career, for the first time in his adult life, in front of subordinates. This is not something that he has ever anticipated happening, and he is at a complete loss on how to proceed. He is off-guard because he doesn't know how much leverage he has with Asher. But he is a politician, and his mind runs almost immediately through all of his options. He settles on reason and persuasion and charm.

"Look, Tom," he says, "we understand how you feel. It's commendable, but there is a way these things must be done."

Asher is having none of it.

"I like that '*we*,'" Asher says. "Me against everyone in the room. But it ain't like that really, is it, Captain? It's just you and me."

Moates looks over to Miller, who is leaning against the closest wall. "Sergeant," he says, "help me out here. Talk some sense into him."

Miller looks at Asher and starts to speak, but then the bloodbath in the Philippines comes back into his mind, with its vision of all those corpses stacked three-deep, just below the lip of Moro Crater. He stops. They had killed women and children that day, *dozens* of them. Maybe *he* hadn't done it, but he was a part of what did. He had sworn then that he would never again be placed in that position, agonizing over the question of whether an individual is responsible for the sins of the group. Yet here he is. He looks over at Moates and then looks away.

Moates shakes his head in disgust and turns back to Asher. "It's just a *corpse*, for God's sake," he says. "It's not even *him*."

"I promised him," Asher says. "I can't explain it, not to *you*, anyway." He pauses, and then says, "I'm taking him back home."

"No, you're not," Moates says. "At least not until we've had an inquest. His death was tragic. It was also completely understandable. He was thought to be reaching for a weapon."

"Bullshit," Asher says. He looks over to Burnett, who is looking only at Moates.

"Everyone who was there agrees that he was reaching for something," Moates says. "It is a reasonable explanation for what happened."

Asher looks around the room, and he cannot tell if everyone is backing Moates, or not. Who knows what has been said, and to whom? Asher feels suddenly very alone.

"This just ain't the way things ought to be," Asher says.

"You need to put away childish things," Moates replies. "This is the way the great world turns. This is the way things *are*. Big difference between *is* and *ought*. Always has been. Always will be."

"Not *always* will be," Asher says. "And anyway, that *ought* comes from somewhere, and I ain't walking all over it, like it ain't even there."

"Well, there's not much you can do about it," Moates replies, "except wait a couple of weeks, and let this blow over. Then you can have your Mexican."

"There *is* something I can do about it," Asher says, hoping that his voice is not betraying his doubts and his fear and that he can pull this off. "I will testify at that inquest as to exactly what happened."

"Damn it, Asher, we wouldn't even be *having* an inquest if you had just been reasonable." Moates pauses for an instant and then says, "It will be your word against theirs, anyway." He motions to the other men in the room.

"Tell you what," Asher says. "Let's just see if all four of them will actually lie under oath."

This strikes a nerve with Moates because he does not know if that would happen. So he pulls the ace out of his sleeve.

"You have other things to consider, Asher," he says evenly. "Like your wife. If this thing gets out of control, her past would be a very visible part of your dismissal. That would be unfortunate."

Asher glances over at Teeter, who is looking at some spot on the carpet in front of him with great interest. His gaze shifts over to Miller, who is looking at Teeter, and then quickly to the whole room, and he realizes that this is not news to at least some of them.

Asher's deep love for Beulah is so strong that a protective instinct rises in him, and he can feel a tremulous anger, waiting there impatiently for him to let it take over.

And then, from nowhere, something curious happens. He feels the rage evaporate. This surprises him because it is not coming volitionally from within himself. He sees the men standing there, and he suddenly understands each one of them. He feels their pride, and he feels their fears, and he knows exactly what makes them act as they do. He feels these things because when he is looking at *them*, he is looking at *himself*. This is what had happened with the old man. He understands them. He understands Teeter, and his desire to please. He understands Miller, and the threat that Asher himself represents to his confidence. He even understands Moates, and he realizes that Moates has the same need for control that Asher had for the laudanum.

He understands all these things, and he is left only with a sense of bittersweet sadness.

"This ain't you," he says to Moates.

"What?" Moates says, startled.

"This ain't really you," Asher repeats. "Just look inside yourself, at what you're doing. You cannot like what you see. You just can't. This ain't what you really want, not down deep, it ain't. Just think about what's right. Think *deep* about it and see it for what it is."

"This is utter nonsense," Moates says.

"Captain," Asher says, reestablishing a sense of the formal order. "I don't want to hurt the Rangers none. They been my life. I ain't going to lie if asked, but I don't care if what happened comes out or not. I mean that. But I also mean to take that poor old man back to his people and see that he ain't just disposed of, like some stray dog."

"That's not going to happen until I say it's going to happen," Moates says firmly, but he senses that this might all be slipping away.

"Captain," Asher says, "I am getting on that train at 5:15 tomorrow morning, and I am taking that old man and his two animals back to Matamoros. I am also stopping in San Diego to pick up the thing he died trying to get to. Not *one* of you have even asked about that. Farrell says he can embalm him tonight if you give him the go-ahead by 6:00. I'll even pay for it, and a coffin. But listen here: if that old man ain't at the depot ready to go by the time I get on that train, then when I get to Brownsville, I am going straight to the Mexican Consulate, and I will raise such hell as you never saw before."

And with that, he turns and leaves.

Asher knows now how the next two days will play out. There are uncertainties, but no doubts.

He needs to talk to Beulah, to get her blessing on the money he will spend, but he must first go back to Farrell's and get a quote on a coffin. He walks the eight blocks back to the funeral home on Fourth Street. Twenty minutes after leaving Moates' office, he enters into the foyer. It is now 1:45. Again, drawn by the sound of the bell over the door, Farrell comes out of his office.

"Show me your coffins," Asher says, and they move down a carpeted corridor to a large showroom, where a dozen coffins are on display.

"We got anything here you could want," Farrell says. "From your basic pine box, which he's already got, to this $900 Mahogany."

"What can I get for fifty dollars?"

"These here," Farrell says, and he points to one wall with three boxes. They are little better than the pine box that Sanchez has now. Asher does not want to feel like he is short-changing the old man.

"Seventy-five dollars," Asher says.

Farrell says, "This one's ninety dollars," and points to a nice dark hardwood casket with a padded fabric interior and round brass bars that run down both sides of the exterior.

"So, a hundred and twenty for the embalming and the box."

Farrell nods.

"I don't know whether Moates is going to allow it," Asher says. "What I'd like to do is this: I will come back here in a little while and write you a check for the full amount. If you get approval by 6:00, do the embalming and have the body at the depot by 4:45 in the morning. If you don't get the go-ahead, please tear up the check."

"A hundred and thirty," Farrell says, and Asher looks at him. Farrell shrugs. "Delivery to the depot before the sun comes up."

Asher hesitates. Beulah is going to come at him with an ax handle. "A hundred and twenty-five," he says, and Farrell nods.

"Is he still dressed?" Asher asks.

"Nope," Farrell says. "Stripped him down when I put him on ice."

"I need to have his clothes cleaned," Asher says.

"Clothes been took," Farrell says. "Last night."

"Moates came for them?"

"No. Ranger. Moates came by to settle up early this morning, and when he found out, he got mad. That's when he told me no one else."

"Describe him please."

"Tall. Mustache. Been drinking. Looks like death kissing a skunk."

Burnett. Asher is worried about the money belt, but there is nothing he can do about that now. He should have kept it.

"I am going to buy some new clothes for him and bring them when I come back with a check," Asher says.

Asher walks back to the hotel. It is 2:30 now, and he fervently hopes that Beulah is in her room off the alley. He does not want to go up those stairs until the day is done.

Beulah is there when Asher walks in. He walks over, kisses the top of her head, and sits down.

"I need to talk to you," he says, and then he tells her of his plan to go to Brownsville, with or without the body, to deliver the crucifix and the two animals to the priest in Matamoros.

"How much?" Beulah asks, always straight to the point.

"Well, a round-trip ticket . . . "

"Just give me the total," Beulah says.

"About forty dollars, I think. For the cross and everything. Unless I get the body."

"Does the cross have Jesus on it?" Beulah asks.

"Yes."

"Then it's a crucifix," Beulah says. "How much *with* the body?"

Asher is quiet, and Beulah says, "The figure isn't going to get any smaller the longer you don't tell me."

"Another one-thirty or so on top of that."

Beulah looks at him with no expression at all. "Help me understand this," she says, with a softness that is starting to frighten him. "We have less than three-hundred dollars saved up, and you're about to lose your job, and you want to spend one-hundred and seventy of it?"

"No, that ain't quite right. I probably *already* lost my job."

"That was funny, sure enough," Beulah says. "Really."

"Thank you," Asher says. "There's something else."

"Teeter spilled the beans," Beulah says. Asher nods, amazed at her, and she shrugs. "Well, we both knew he was going to. And now Moates is using that to try to get what he wants." She is quiet for a moment, and then she says, "Thomas, you do what you have to do. I mean that. We'll just have to start over someplace else."

"Probably," Asher says.

"I've heard Odessa is nice," Beulah says, and they both laugh.

Asher stands, kisses her on the forehead again, and walks to the door. Then he turns to her and says, "Could I get you to get some clothes for the Mexican and get them over to Farrell's? Just some pants and a shirt. New, and clean."

She nods, and then he pauses for a moment and says something that takes her breath away.

"Beulah," he says, looking down at the hat in his hands, and then his voice trails off. She knows that words do not come easily to him, and she waits patiently. He looks back up at her.

"The day will come when you will close my eyes to this world forever," he says. "Looking at your sweet face will be a wonderful way to leave. You've given my life purpose, and hope." He pauses, and starts to say something else, but then he doesn't, and he turns and leaves.

Beulah will outlive Asher by eight years, and every night of those eight years, as she lays her gray head on her pillow, she will remember the sight of him standing at that door and saying the words to her that will give her as much solace as both Holy Writ and *Middlemarch*.

Asher goes to the Western Union Office, where he sends out two telegrams. The first is 23 words long ($1.15), and it asks Father Pedro Bard to be at the depot in San Diego tomorrow morning at 11:00, with the crucifix, and that Asher will pay the freight. The second one is to Father Roberto Valdez, in Matamoros, Mexico, through the Western Union Office in Brownsville. It is 44 words long ($2.20), and it tells that priest who he is and that he will be coming into Brownsville at 1:00 Tuesday morning, and that it concerns the death of Emilio Sanchez, and to please bring a few men with him. He does not mention specifically the casket, or the crucifix, or the animals.

From there, he goes to the livery stable and makes arrangements to pick up Sanchez's horse and pack mule, and all of his gear, at 4:30 in the morning. He asks how much is owed.

"Nothing," the proprietor says. "It's on the Rangers' open account."

Finally, he goes back to Farrell's with a check. As he fills it out, sitting in the visitor's chair at Farrell's desk, the undertaker picks up a sack from the floor beside him and says, "Your wife brought these by a few minutes ago."

Asher removes from the sack a pair of white cotton pants and a white shirt. He stares at them, transfixed, and reality now begins the process of shifting on him, ever so subtly.

These are the same clothes that Sanchez was wearing in the dream he had on the train yesterday afternoon.

Farrell can see that Asher has been affected in some way by the garments, and he is curious. "Is everything all right?" he asks.

"Yes, it is," Asher says.

10

Morose after Asher leaves, Moates is left with a room full of men and nothing to say. Miller watches him stare wordlessly at the door Asher has just exited, and he is struck by the expression of complete shock on Moates' face. Finally, Moates says, "I guess that's it. We all know what's at stake here."

When Miller thinks on it later, it occurs to him that Moates is afraid to pursue any conversation with his men that might result in discovering that they are not all of one mind.

Miller files out with the rest of them and walks dejectedly to his cottage home on Crockett Street. He enters and removes his coat and puts it on the rack in the vestibule, and then goes into the dining room and sits at the table. It is not quite 2:00. Leona comes from the kitchen with two cups of coffee and sits down across from him. She sees on his face the weight of the world.

"It's time, Horace. Every detail," she says, and so he tells her everything he knows, and answers truthfully every question she asks. As he speaks, he slowly gains some measure of the moral clarity he has been searching for, and a resulting sense of direction.

He tells her of the old man's shooting, and he tells her of the uncertainty and fear that he felt, and he tells her of the wretchedness of his behavior that followed. He tells her of his first suggestion to Asher regarding ending the old man's suffering. He tells her of his second suggestion to Asher regarding the shovel. He tells her of his flight from the dying man. He tells her of Moates' threat concerning Asher's wife. He tells her all of it and answers all of her questions, and as he does so, he hopes fervently that his candor will be regarded by her as virtue. Nothing in this world is as important to him as her respect for him.

Leona offers her counsel, and then there is nothing left to say. She sits quietly, with the cup of coffee in her hands, while Miller goes to the telephone on the hallway wall and goes through the switchboard to call the District Office. He informs Moates that he is on his way back over. He does not allow Moates an opportunity to decline but puts the earpiece back in its cradle. He glances at Leona, and she wonders if the doubt she sees on his face reflects a concern for career or a desire for righteousness. Both, probably. She understands that neither good things nor bad things are done without some mixture of motivations.

"You *do* understand what this may mean?" Miller asks her.

"No, probably not," Leona replies. "But I do understand what it means to your integrity if you continue to let that man pressure you into doing this despicable thing."

Miller says nothing because he knows that there is no answer to this. Frustrated, he looks away from her and shakes his head.

"Horace," Leona says, "if Asher does what he says he is going to do, the prudent thing for Moates to do would be precisely what I have suggested. If he decides against that, then the prudent thing for *you* to do would be to buck him. Asher *is* going to follow through on this."

"Maybe he will," Miller says, "and maybe he won't."

"He will," Leona says, "because he is on the side of the angels."

And so, thirty-five minutes later, Moates and Miller are sitting at Moates' desk back in the District Office. Their conversation is not at all pleasant, and Moates has just shut the inner door.

"So, what are you proposing we do?" Moates asks. He is not even attempting to disguise his anger.

"I am not *proposing* anything," Miller replies. "I am *telling* you that we are going to own up to all of this. We're going to have to."

Moates stands and walks over to the large bay window on the other side of the pool table, with its expansive view of downtown Laredo. He leans forward, his forehead lightly touching the cold glass.

"Miller," he says, "I can't tell you how much your leadership on this has disappointed me. This whole thing has been mismanaged from the very beginning."

Finally, there it is: the fear and frustration are finally out in the open, and Miller is glad of it. He resolves to speak evenly and rationally and to hold his volcanic apprehensions in check.

"I think that there is plenty of blame to go around," Miller says. "The fact is, the main cause of this whole thing was Burnett's drinking. I made it clear to you that he didn't have my confidence, but you forced him on me, anyway. I don't understand why you protect him."

"He saved my life in Cuba," Moates says, and he turns to regard Miller with great sadness. "This is going to destroy him."

This answer startles Miller. "I didn't know that," he says. He considers it for a moment and then concludes that this may be an adequate explanation, but it is not a satisfactory excuse. And then another notion strikes Miller so suddenly that it drives away all other thoughts.

"Captain," he says, "you're actually disappointed that we found nothing out there, aren't you? You *wanted* a violent confrontation. But the fact is, we had no business being out there. None."

Moates avoids the question. "Ah, the convenience of hindsight. We didn't make this world the way it is, and we don't make the rules."

Miller, like Asher, is struck by Moates' use of the word 'we,' but instead of challenging it, he embraces it. The clarity he has been looking for seems as though it is right in front of him now.

"But we *did* make the rules, in a way," Miller answers. "We *both* did, as we went along. And the world is the worse for it."

"Self-righteous crap," Moates says, shaking his head.

"Fine," Miller says. "What would you have had me do?"

"Just about anything but what you've done."

"What should I have done, then? Just gone ahead and killed the poor wretch myself? Swear the men to secrecy?"

There is no answer to this. Moates has turned back to the window.

Then, something unexpected: "Shit," Moates says suddenly, and with great vehemence. This is so unlike Moates that for an instant Miller thinks that it is in response to what he has just said. But then Moates stands back from the glass and squares his shoulders, as if preparing himself to go on stage, and Miller realizes that he is reacting to something that he sees outside. Miller rises and joins Moates at the window.

"*You* brought him here, didn't you?" Moates asks.

Miller is looking intently now at the traffic on the street outside, and he can see nothing. He glances over to Moates and then follows his seething gaze and now sees, quite clearly, the tall, imposing figure of Edward Smith walking along the sidewalk toward them. He is obviously coming from the train depot, and he carries a small valise.

"No," Miller says, "it wasn't me." But he is thinking that if you remove Teeter and Burnett from consideration, it could have been either Asher *or* Anspach. Leona is right: there is no avoiding this.

Curiously, Moates feels buoyed by Miller's denial. Perhaps Smith's visit here is unrelated to the Sanchez debacle. But then a new thought comes to him: whatever Smith *is* here for, Moates cannot control the conversation if Miller is present.

"I need you to leave," Moates says. "Now."

Miller turns and retrieves his coat and wordlessly walks out of the room. He is frustrated because he wishes to be there to defend himself if Moates attempts to shift responsibility. And then he feels a sad and introspective anger because he instinctively loathes the transactional ways of thinking and acting that have been present since the moment of the Mexican's shooting.

Smith enters the building and he and Miller pass each other in the foyer. Smith tips his hat and says, "Sergeant, how are you?" But he does not pause for pleasantries and moves on into Moates' office, where he shuts the door behind him.

When Smith enters, Moates is standing in the middle of the room, arm extended. "Ed, what a delightful surprise."

Edward H. Smith is the captain of Company C, which is a one-man investigation unit. Although he has been a contract detective for the Rangers in the past, he has only been a sworn Ranger for a few months. Moates has known him, though, for some years, and loathes him viscerally. He finds Smith to be an overbearing jackass, educated but coarse. Their relationship has always been curt and formal, but Smith has the favor of both the new governor, Ferguson, and the new adjutant general, Hutchings, and Moates is wary of getting the conversation off to a bad start.

Smith shakes his hand in a very perfunctory way, and then takes off his coat and hat, and sits down in the chair opposite Moates' side of the desk. Moates also sits down, examining Smith's face closely. He can discern nothing.

Smith gets right to the point. "What's happening here?"

Smith's abruptness startles Moates, but its ambiguous phrasing gives him hope that the question is general, and not specific.

"Nothing beyond the ordinary," he says, as breezily as he can.

Smith regards him for a moment, sighs theatrically, and rises back up to his feet and walks back over to the chair where his coat and hat and valise rest. "Well, Render, I was hoping that we could have a good, honest conversation here, but I can see that's not in the offing."

Moates, with low-level panic beginning to rise in him, tries to salvage the exchange. "Oh, you mean the Sanchez situation?" He tries to make this sound off-hand, as though it has just occurred to him, but he knows that it has come out awkwardly and insincerely, and he is embarrassed to the point of blushing.

Smith regards Moates, coat and hat in hand. "Was that his name?"

"Yes. Emilio Sanchez," Moates says. "If you will tell me what you have heard, I can try to bring your understanding of the situation up to date."

Smith is surprised by Moates' lack of finesse and is vexed by his stonewalling. "Assume I know nothing," he says, which isn't true, in any sense at all. Before noon on Saturday, the previous day, Archibald Parr had called Hutchings. "Something I think you need to know," Parr had said, as though he were doing Hutchings a great service, when in fact he was only selling Moates down the river, as a favor, it turns out, to Amos Beauchamp. But what Hutchings heard was enough to know that he needed Smith to pay a surprise visit to Moates. So here he is, on his one day off, in Laredo, which he considers to be the ass-end of nowhere.

"Well, mistakes were certainly made," Moates is saying. "I am trying to determine fully what happened in order to assess our next step."

"'Mistakes were certainly made,'" Smith repeats in a crude mimicry. He smiles, and looks down, and shakes his head. "Do you know what the passive voice is, Render?"

"Yes, of course."

"Well, if you insult my intelligence by using it one more time, this conversation is over." He looks back up at Moates, smiling, but the look is withering. "Now tell me what the hell is going on," he says.

"Well, Ed," Moates says, completely intimidated now, "you seem to know quite a bit already. What is *your* interest in all this?" Moates, playing his instinctive games, is grasping at jurisdiction to take control of the conversation. He knows that he and Smith are peers, at least on paper. He knows that he does not want to get into a pissing contest with Edward H. Smith. And he knows that this technicality is his last hope.

"Hutchings has sent me here to get the truth about the Mexican's death," Smith says, and then he pauses for a moment to take a furtive delight in the utter defeat that is crossing Moates' face.

There is an awkward silence, and Smith suddenly feels like a cat toying with his food. He decides to ease up on Moates a bit before the son of a bitch just shuts down on him. He has expected to encounter resistance of some sort, but this has been like taking candy from a baby.

"I think I know what happened in the field," Smith says. "Those things *can* happen, but they need to be dealt with immediately and properly. What I need to know is what's happened *since* then."

"I have been trying to contain the situation," Moates says. "This could have been kept under wraps, but one of the Rangers is trying to use it for leverage. He was about to be dismissed, and now this."

Moates' voice trails off, and Smith walks back over to Moates' desk, and sits back down, still holding his coat and hat and valise.

"Render, talk to me. What were your men even *doing* out there?"

"We received a telegram from Headquarters," Moates says. "Late Tuesday night."

"I saw that telegram," Smith says. "It should never have gone out." Having said this, Smith immediately laughs at himself, inwardly. *Now,* who is using the passive voice? A man who reports to the man who *sent* that telegram, *that's* who is using the passive voice.

"I just wanted to get a jump on whatever it might be," Moates says.

"Render, you have made a mess of things. You wanted political visibility. Well, now you've got it."

"There was nothing out there," Moates says. He looks away, wistfully. "It was all for nothing."

"If it's any consolation to you," Smith says, "we are going to go back and see exactly how all this happened. Not just your part of this mess, but the whole ball of wax."

Smith sighs and gets to his feet and again walks back over to the door with his coat and hat and valise. He turns to look at Moates.

"Render, I've never particularly liked you," he says. "You are excessively ambitious, and your leadership on this has been . . . " He trails off, unwilling to commit to the opinion. "You have overreached," he says finally. "Get this damned thing cleaned up, and cleaned up well, and then you and Hutchings can sit down and discuss your future."

After Smith leaves, Render Moates sits for the longest time looking at the closed door and finally acknowledges his own fallibility. It is not a *moral* inventory he is taking at this juncture, but a *tactical* one. He replays in his mind every decision he has made and every action he has taken, and he grades them against the situation that has resulted. His mind goes back to what Asher had said to him, not four hours before. "Look inside yourself," Asher had said. Moates honestly tries to consider these words now, but they are still incomprehensible to him.

At length, he rises and puts out the lights, and goes home. He retires into his den, starts a fire in the beautiful stone fireplace, gets a crystal decanter of whiskey and a matching crystal glass, and then sits in his beautiful leather armchair, staring at the fire for hours in the darkness, the flames flickering on his face.

Does the embered glow help his introspection? Does the alcohol help to insulate him from consideration of the interruption of the very flow of his life? Is there anything that can help him hide from himself?

At 10:00, the sound of the grandfather clock in the entryway echoes through the house, and to Moates, it sounds like a valediction. He has been considering all the different ways the next week might go, and he cannot, for the life of him, see himself coming out unscathed.

At 11:15, he hears the bell at the front door, and he rises quickly and makes his way to the vestibule. His wife is asleep, and he does not want her awakened, because he does not want to talk to her. It is Horace Miller, standing there with Gerald Anspach, and the three of them stand there in the cold doorway and talk quietly for a few minutes. Then the two men leave, and Moates returns to his den.

He is in profound despair.

At half-past seven the sun sets, and the light begins to fade, and twenty minutes later the automatic street lights come on, and Sunday draws to a close.

Edward Smith is moving on to Del Rio the following day to swear in some new Rangers. It is an indirect train route there, and he cannot leave until the 7:40 rolls north-east the next morning. He checks into the Sirocco Hotel and gets a very fine room on the second floor, and then has dinner at the hotel restaurant. After he finishes, he attends the evening service at the Baptist church right off the plaza. He enjoys such times as these because he gets a clandestine satisfaction from the occasional recognition he gets from complete strangers. After the service, he returns to his room and retires early. He thinks no more of Moates or of anything to do with the dead Mexican. There will be plenty of time for the inevitable blame game later.

Cord Burnett spends the evening at Delgado's Saloon, numbing himself to the uncertainties of his future. The alcohol makes it easier for him to think about the possibility of taking some sort of vengeance on Thomas Asher. At the meeting in the District Office earlier that afternoon, he had seen Asher break Moates, which he did not think was possible. He knows now that Asher will not let things drop, and he cannot see a way forward that does not involve him taking the blame for the Mexican's death. Such is his simmering panic that he had gone to Farrell's the night before and taken possession of the old man's clothes. His thinking had been to destroy them so that there was less evidence. It was drunken thinking. What difference did the bullet hole in the clothes make, when there was still a *body* with a bullet hole in it?

Is he to blame? He doesn't think so. It was an accident, for God's sake. It could happen to anyone. Such is his thinking, and such is his night. When Delgado's closes at 2:00, he finds himself standing in the quiet street, wondering dully what his next move is.

Horace Miller comes back to his small house after his meeting with Moates, to find that Leona has stepped out. He has a plan now fixed firmly in his mind, but he will not act on it until he talks to her.

He sits at their dining table and considers all of the pain and uncertainty he has allowed into his life by not seeking her counsel earlier. He had sat on the self-revulsion engendered by that terrible thing in the Philippines for two years before he finally told her of it. He had resigned his commission in the army, and flailed about for over a year, looking for some position that matched his talents and his temperament, and had ultimately dragged her and their little girl to Laredo, because he thought he had found it with the Texas Rangers. The optimism he had felt at West Point is a distant memory.

After a while, Leona returns home, and again sits across from him, and asks about his meeting with Moates. He recounts to her how badly it went, and of Edward Smith's arrival, and he then tells her what he thinks he should do, if she is agreeable. She tells him then that she has been to see Beulah Asher, and what a fine woman she seems to have become, and how unfair it is for her to have to suffer what she is about to endure. Of course, she agrees with his course of action.

Gerald Anspach is a bachelor and is enjoying a quiet evening at his room in the hotel, reading a novel by Frank Norris about farmers contending with the railroad. The meeting at Moates' office has unsettled him because he has never before seen Moates so much out of his element. Anspach has considered his own conduct relative to what has happened to the Mexican and has concluded that it has been exemplary and that he is safe from any repercussions. He loves being a Texas Ranger, so he had resolved earlier to take Miller's lead in what to do. If Miller had decided that burying their mistake would be the best course of action, that would be okay with him. He wouldn't particularly like it, but he could live with it. He is, therefore, more than a little surprised when Miller knocks on his door just a little after 10:30.

At 1:00, Render Moates' wife awakens and notices his empty side of the bed. She had heard him come in, hours ago. Curious, she arises and goes to the head of the stairs and sees lights flickering from beneath the closed door of his den. She goes down and raps gently on the door. After a moment, she gently opens it.

He is staring at the glow in the fireplace, lost in thought.

"Render," she says. "What is it?"

"Well, Maudie," he says, "I seem to have made a complete mess of things." He looks up at her. For the first time in many years, she sees vulnerability and uncertainty. She moves to him, kneels in front of the chair, reaches up, and takes his head into her arms.

Lyle Teeter sits in his room at the hotel reading a dime novel, unconcerned about anything but whether the fictional lawman is going to both vanquish the villain *and* get the girl.

When Thomas Asher finishes the arrangements for the next morning with Farrell, he goes back to the hotel and sees that the door to Beulah's room off the alley is closed. He then laboriously works his way up the staircase to their room. To his surprise, Beulah is not there.

He stares for a time at the unopened bottle of laudanum, still sitting on the table where Beulah had placed it the previous afternoon. He feels very tempted, but he leaves it alone. He is completely spent, and now that there is nothing left for him to do, he feels his body winding down. He considers sleep and looks at the bed, but the thought of what the soft mattress would do to his back without laudanum frightens him. So he lies down face-up on the floor by his bed and drifts off. This is how Beulah finds him when she returns to the room an hour later.

She lets him sleep for a while, but toward the middle of the evening, she awakens him to get him into bed. She helps him into a sitting position on the floor and then helps him up to the side of the bed. He slowly comes back to wakefulness.

"You weren't here," he says.

"I was at church," Beulah says. "Listen, there is something I have needed to tell you. Leona Miller came to see me."

"Miller's wife?" Asher says. "When?"

"Thursday. And then at church tonight, she told me what her husband told her about what Moates did today. Thomas, she *sat* with me."

"What did you tell her on Thursday?"

"Everything," Beulah says. "Word was all over town. She is a very fine person, and I think she can help defend us."

"Can't be done," Asher says. He shakes his head. "Teeter didn't even make it to the train without talking. Must have told Hardesty."

"You don't think people can accept it?"

"Beulah," Asher says, "people like feeling superior too much. They won't *never* accept this. We'll have to leave here. There ain't no way out of it." She considers this for a moment, and then grudgingly agrees.

"Did you make your arrangements?" she asks.

"As many as I could," Asher says. "We just have to see how tomorrow plays out."

She undresses him, and gives him some aspirin, and puts him to bed. This act inflames in her the longing for him that is always there, and she opens herself to him with the desire to receive him, to become one. It seems to her the most beautiful and natural thing in the world. She is practiced, and she knows how to do this without hurting him.

He loves her dearly and desires the same union and at first, he responds, but then he gently disengages. He cannot stop thinking about the old Mexican, lying on ice over at Farrell's.

"I can't, Beulah," he says. "Not right now, anyway."

"Why?" she asks.

"Wouldn't seem right," Asher says.

11

At three-thirty in the morning, Beulah's alarm goes off, and she helps Asher rise and get ready.

While Asher comes awake, Beulah disappears for ten minutes and then returns, carrying a large, heavy porcelain bowl full of hot water. She puts it on the dresser under the mirror and reaches into a drawer for a bar of soap and a straight razor, which she strops sharp for him. She leaves these and a rag by the bowl.

As Asher cleans and shaves, she goes to a wardrobe and pulls down his other suit, now cleaned and pressed, and lays it out on the bed. Then she sits at the table and watches her husband. The laudanum bottle is still there, unopened.

In the mirror, Asher sees her glance at it, and he says, "It is still sealed. The druggist may refund the money."

She regards him, and he nods, and she puts the bottle in her purse.

He finishes at the washbasin and dries his face and begins to dress. He transfers everything from his dirty suit on the floor by the bed to his clean one, including his badge and, Beulah sees, an old newspaper.

When he is ready, she walks over to him and uses the flat of her hand to caress a few wrinkles out of his coat and pants. She looks into his eyes as she does this and she sees a fatigue that looks as if it has no bottom. She thinks that he is, at this moment, the most beautiful man she has ever seen.

He pulls a traveling bag from the wardrobe and opens it, and then takes his gun and holster from where they hang on the post at the foot of the bed and wraps the gun belt around the Colt and puts it into the bag. To this, he adds a few toiletries, and then he shuts the bag.

"I need three things," he says. "First, I need some cash."

She walks over to the dresser and pulls a metal cookie box from a drawer, and opens it, and holds it out to him. Inside are some greenbacks and a few silver dollars. He takes the greenbacks, about thirty dollars in all, looking at her as he does so. She doesn't flinch.

"I also need a few blank bank drafts," he says, and she tears three new ones from the ledger book on the dresser and hands them to him. He folds them and puts them in his wallet.

"And I need a pencil and some paper." She goes again to the dresser and hands him the items.

He regards her for a moment, and neither of them speaks. Then he kisses her on the forehead. "It's almost over," he says.

He pauses at the door, regards her for a moment, and leaves.

Beulah moves over to the bay window, and after a few moments, he appears on the street below her and walks away. She can see his pain as he walks, and she watches until he disappears across the plaza.

Asher walks to the livery stable and is dismayed to see that it is dark. He tries in vain to raise someone, anyone, but the place is deserted. Then he goes to the corral to look for the two animals. They are not there. He suspects that Moates has taken them away somewhere, and he is furious. In the likely event that the body has not been released, he will have to be content now with taking only the crucifix to Matamoros.

Now he walks to the train station, goes inside, and there is no trace of either Farrell or the casket. He moves out onto the depot itself. The train is there, and he is profoundly disappointed, at first glance, not to find anything that he had hoped to see. But almost immediately he hears his name called, and he looks to his left, down toward the freight area, and he is relieved, almost to the point of tears.

Miller is standing there, motioning gently with his hand for Asher to come to him. Anspach is standing beside him.

And in front of them, on a wheeled gurney, is the casket that Asher had ordered from Farrell's fourteen hours before.

Asher walks over to them and finds that they are smiling, and he realizes that they want him to be pleased. He shakes their hands warmly.

"Well, here he is," Miller says.

"Moates gave in?" Asher asks.

"Yes," Miller says. "It was late last night, but it all got done. Farrell was up half the night getting the old man ready. He's angry, but money is money."

"Well . . ." Asher says, and shrugs. He starts to say something further when something occurs to him.

"Say, I have got to get this onto a freight car," he says, touching the casket with his hand. "I need to go make the arrangements."

"It's been done," Miller says and hands him a bill of lading. "One way to Brownsville."

"It's been paid for?" Asher asks.

"We split the cost," Anspach says.

"We also split the cost of the embalming and the casket," Miller says, and hands Asher the bank draft that Asher had written to Farrell the previous afternoon. Asher detects an odd pride in Miller's voice, and he realizes now that he is no longer alone in any of this.

"I'll get the station master to help," Anspach says, and steps away.

Asher regards Miller for a moment, and it becomes clear to him that he is seeing the true Miller now, the inward Miller, and he regrets the doubts he has had for the last three days.

"This is such a relief," Asher says. "I can't tell you."

"For me too," Miller responds.

"There ain't no conditions on this?" Asher asks.

"None," Miller says.

Anspach returns with a freight agent, and Asher explains to him, "We need to get this casket onto a freight car." The agent looks at the bill of lading and then moves away for a moment to secure extra help.

Something new occurs to Asher. "Was it you that picked up the old man's horses from the livery stable?"

"Yes," Miller says.

"And their freight is paid?"

Miller points to the bill of lading in Asher's hand and nods. "They are already on one of the stock cars, along with the old man's gear."

A freight car is open, and they roll the casket over to the door. The station master gets three other men, and together they all lift the casket and laboriously move it into the car and set it down on the floor on the far side. While they are doing this, Asher goes back into the depot and buys a round-trip ticket to Brownsville.

Finally, the three of them walk to a passenger car, and Asher mounts the steps and turns to face them.

"One last thing," Miller says. "Burnett is angry and scared. He's been drinking since yesterday afternoon after the meeting and was at Delgado's until they closed. I can't find him anywhere. Be careful."

Asher nods, and Anspach tips his hat and turns away. Miller stays and extends his hand.

"Thank you," he says. "From the bottom of my heart." And that is it. Miller steps back from the car, and Asher steps up to find a seat.

In 1,164 days, Horace Miller will be lying on a stretcher on the floor of a field hospital tent near the small French village of Le Theolet. Outside, he will hear an artillery barrage supporting the Allied advance into Belleau Wood. A triage surgeon will wander by and bend over to examine his wounds. Miller will see him raise his eyes back up to him and say, "I'm very sorry, Major," and give him some morphine. Miller will accept this calmly and smile ruefully. He will bleed out in less than an hour, and three memories will give him tremendous solace and pride in those final moments: the afternoon that he married Leona Barstow in Goshen, New York; the evening that his daughter was born in Hardin, Kentucky; and the morning that he delivered the body of Emilio Sanchez to Thomas Asher at the train depot in Laredo, Texas.

When the train pulls into San Diego at 11:00, Asher exits the passenger car and finds Father Bard on the depot siding.

"I didn't see your telegram until about an hour ago," the priest says. He points behind him to a wagon at the side of the depot. There, completely unpacked and unprepared, and hanging off the back, rests the crucifix. There are two laborers sitting on the buckboard. "I haven't had time to make any arrangements at all," the priest says.

Asher and the priest walk into the depot. Just inside the door, Father Bard touches Asher's elbow to stop him for a moment. "Let me do the talking," he says. "Gordon Nader is a parishioner, but he can be . . . difficult."

The station master is sitting in his office, and he looks up when they enter. The priest immediately begins the conversation.

"Gordon, I need a favor. The crucifix from the chapel is out on the parish wagon, and we need to send it to Brownsville, today."

"I thought *they* were going to do this," Nader says.

"And they are," the priest replies, "through this gentleman right here. Mr. Asher. He's with the Texas Rangers."

Nader assesses Asher for the briefest of glances and then says to the priest, "Well, it can't be today. No time to do the paperwork."

"Gordon, help us out here," Father Bard says.

Nader sighs, and stands, and says, "Where is it?"

The three men walk out to the wagon. "Good Lord," Nader says. "This thing isn't even packed up."

"Does it need to be?" Asher asks.

"Hell, yes," Nader replies. "Not only that, but the Jesus has got to be taken off the cross. He'll break otherwise."

"Look, Gordon, please. It is probably now or never. Can't we just put it carefully into a freight car? Mr. Asher is going on to Brownsville with it. He'll watch over it."

"Can't go in the freight car like *that*," Nader says. "It'll break."

"I *could* ride in the freight car with it," Asher says. "I can watch over it."

"No, you couldn't," Nader says. "Against the rules."

Father Bard notices an opening in what the station master has just said, and he jumps on it.

"Gordon, Mr. Asher can ride in the passenger car. As far as getting it there, we could waive all liability, right on the Bill of Lading."

Frustrated now, Nader regards the priest for a moment, and then asks, "How much does this thing weigh?"

"I have no idea," the priest says.

So the four men, with the station master watching, unload the crucifix and place it on a commercial freight scale near the wagon. "Two hundred and sixty-five pounds," Nader says.

They march back into his office, and Nader pulls out a rate book and eyeballs in his mind the dimensions of the crucifix, and finally says, "It would cost you $17.70."

Asher says, "I can't spare that much cash. Can you take a bank draft?" He has the blank checks Beulah has given him, in his wallet.

"Not from out of town," Nader says, and smiles, vindicated.

"Just a moment," the priest says. "I have the cash. Mr. Asher can write the parish a check."

The stationmaster sighs and finally acknowledges defeat. He writes up a bill of lading and takes the cash from Father Bard, and Asher hands the priest a check. Nader writes on the Bill of Lading, "The Road assumes no liability for condition," and makes both Father Bard and Asher sign the sender's copy, the receiver's copy, and Asher's.

They get the crucifix loaded, and Asher says good-bye to the priest, and he gets back on the passenger car just as the train pulls out of San Diego, headed for Corpus Christi. Asher can finally relax a little.

He now has everything aboard that he could have hoped for, and the only thing remaining to worry about is making sure that everything is transferred to the southbound train for the last leg of the trip to Brownsville. He watches the scenery go by under the afternoon sun, and gradually he fades into a sleep as deep as his back will allow.

He dreams again, and this time he is standing on a mountainside stubbled with charred trees. There is a young man standing near him, who regards him thoughtfully for a moment and then says, with a radiant smile, "Something wonderful is coming." Asher awakens and sits thinking on this for a time. He is utterly baffled.

At ten minutes past three, the train pulls into Robstown. Asher exits the passenger car, walks down to the freight section of the train, and watches to be certain that everything that needs to come off the train actually *does* come off. The crucifix is unloaded first because it has been loaded into the car last, and Asher notes the consternation of the station agent as he finds it in its raw, unpacked state, with only a copy of the bill of lading tacked to it. Once the crucifix is safely off the train, Asher decides not to deal with the agent until he must, when the crucifix will need to go onto a southbound freight car.

The casket comes off a different freight car with no trouble, and they take it inside the depot on a rolling cart. Asher supposes this to be a station policy, to avoid upsetting people.

Finally, the horse and pack mule are brought off a stock car, and Asher breathes easily for a few moments, until he realizes that he has not seen the old man's gear, including the two saddles. He quickly finds the station agent and tells him of his concern, and the two men move sequentially along the freight cars, looking for the gear. They find it in the fourth car, void of any identifying documentation whatsoever. The station agent sighs, and he and a depot laborer get the gear unloaded to the depot platform just before the train moves on to Corpus Christi.

It is still at least two hours before the train will pull out of Robstown, and Asher goes into the station café and orders a cup of coffee and a piece of apple pie. He then returns to the depot, and sits on a bench in the afternoon sun, and takes some aspirin, and waits.

At 5:20, the train headed to Brownsville pulls in from the north. Asher has figured out how to proceed, but he only has twenty minutes.

He finds the station agent and shows his badge and says, "I need your help."

The agent looks at him, and Asher can sense immediate resistance. "With what?" the man asks, not even attempting to mask his irritation.

"I need the casket in the depot, and that cross, and the two saddles and the gear we unloaded earlier all placed on the same freight car going to Brownsville," he says. "And there's a horse and a pack mule in your corral that need to be on one of them stock cars."

"It's a crucifix," the station agent says.

"Yes, a crucifix," Asher says.

"Is that all?" the agent asks sarcastically.

"No," Asher says. "I also need to be able to ride in the freight car."

The agent laughs and shakes his head. "No. Company policy."

Asher reaches into his coat pocket and retrieves his wallet. Carefully, to avoid attention, he opens the wallet and pulls out a five-dollar bill, which he holds in his hand.

"You can't be serious," the station agent says.

Asher retrieves another five. Ten minutes later, the horse and mule are on the stock car, and the casket and the gear have been loaded on the freight car, but the crucifix won't fit.

"No room," says the station agent.

"Can't we tie the cross to the top of the car?" Asher asks.

"No possible way," the station agent says. "And it's a crucifix."

Both Asher and the station agent look down at Asher's wallet.

The train has ramped up to full speed now, and Asher has lit an oil lantern, and its light fills the inside of the freight car. He has sat down on the floor, back against the wall of the car. His right hand rests gently on the casket. He prays for the soul of Emilio Sanchez, and part of him wonders if he is just talking to himself. But he feels a peace now, and a sense of fulfillment, and he imagines the old man lying in the box as if he is fully aware of Asher's presence and grateful for it.

After a time, Asher gets to his feet. The pain in the small of his back is increasing steadily, and there is no relief for it. It is always present, but he realizes how much more content he is with the pain than he was with the ability to ease that pain but suffer instead from the need for the laudanum.

There is a large wooden crate of Andrews Tractor parts that would serve as a good desk. It is far too heavy to move, so he goes over to it and places the lantern on it, in the center. Then he drags another smaller box over to it and sits down on it.

There is something that he feels he must do before he arrives in Brownsville and before he meets the priest from Matamoros. He reaches into his jacket pocket and pulls out the folded newspaper with Sanchez's transcribed words scribbled in the margins. Then he reaches into his shirt pocket and pulls out the several folded sheets of clean paper that he has brought with him, and the sharpened pencil.

He is very uneasy about whether he can recreate the sequence in which he wrote everything down, and he does not want to read haltingly and phonetically everything he has written aloud, fumbling to figure out what is next, as the priest listens. He wants to transcribe everything now and simply hand the priest the complete, linear message, with as little uncertainty as possible. He is very much afraid of making a mistake that would prevent the priest from understanding whatever it was that Sanchez wanted to tell him. He pulls his spectacles from his vest pocket.

He spreads the clean sheets of paper on the box, picks up the pencil, and begins to copy what he has written down. He starts at the quarter-page advertisement and writes very slowly and very carefully, using block letters. As he hits the end of a margin, he follows the drawn arrow to the next margin, where the text continues. Only once in the process does he find that he had forgotten to point carefully to the next margin, but he is able to find with some certainty where the text continues. This process takes an hour, and two of the three sheets. He then spends another half-hour going back over it, cross-checking it carefully. Finally, he is satisfied that it is as accurate as he can make it.

He carefully folds the transcribed sheets and puts them in his shirt pocket. Then he refolds the newspaper and puts it carefully back into his inside jacket pocket. Finally, he lowers the level of light in the lantern and sits back carefully against the wall of the car.

It is still several hours until he arrives in Brownsville, and he cannot seem to get emotionally comfortable with the enforced idleness. Even though so much has happened, everything is still unresolved somehow in his mind. Asher wants only for the next twelve hours to be over.

After a little while, he stands up and wanders over to the door of the car. It is cold inside, to the point of frosted breath, but the car still feels stuffy. Asher hesitates for a moment and then pulls the handle to the sliding freight door up and over, and slowly slides the door to the right. A blast of frigid air enters the car, but the sight that presents itself to him is so unexpectedly beautiful that he takes a step to his left so that he is out of the airstream.

The south Texas landscape is gliding by, under a full moon, which rides high in the heavens. There is not a cloud in the sky. The whole tableau in front of him, despite its inherent ambiance of arid desolation, seems indescribably beautiful. Everything is bathed with a light blue glow, and Asher feels as though he is in another world. It is not a world that he finds unsettling; it instead presents itself to him as a place of peace, and quiet joy. Asher wonders why he perceives it this way, and he senses slowly that his perception feels like more than an emotional reaction, and that it has some measure of truth behind it. This comforts him because he is weary of having no confidence in his thoughts.

He is suddenly aware of a moving moon-shadow on the ground in front of him, paralleling the movement of the train and beginning to merge with his own shadow on the ground, which is being cast by the light of the lantern behind him. The shadow is moving at the same speed as the train, and at first, Asher thinks that it must be some kind of bird. But the size precludes that. Asher leans out of the car, holding his hat firmly down on his head, and looks up.

There, clearly visible in the moonlight, is a bi-winged aero-plane. He cannot hear it over the sounds of locomotion, but it is flying, intentionally it seems, directly over the train several hundred feet in the air, almost directly over his freight car. Beulah almost let him go up in one at a fair in Galveston the previous year, but she finally decided that she did not want to spend the four dollars. As a result, Asher can only imagine what things must look like from that altitude. He tries to imagine what the train, and the desert landscape, must seem like to the pilot, and then it occurs to him that it may not be just the train the pilot is following, but the very car he stands in. He pictures in his mind what the crucifix mounted to the top of the car must seem like, moving across the landscape, bathed in moonlight, and he wonders what the pilot must be experiencing. He also supposes that the pilot can see the waters of the Gulf off to his left, and he imagines the sight to be wondrous.

At length, the cold and the wind begin to take their toll, and Asher steps back and slides the door closed and returns to his seat on the box, and lies down beside it, on his back. For the next two-and-a-half hours, he alternately dozes and stares quietly at the dim light of the lantern.

He is dozing when the sound of the locomotive horn sounds, and he wakes to feel the train beginning to slow down. He pulls his pocket watch from his vest and sees that they must be coming into Brownsville. He stands up and brushes the dirt from his clothes. He looks over to the casket and starts to say something aloud to Emilio, but then he checks himself. Instead, he walks over and slowly slides open the door.

The city is gliding by as the train slows. There is a foundry, then storage buildings, and finally the beginning of the freight yard. He glances forward and sees the depot coming up, and notices immediately a group of half a dozen men standing on the platform, staring in the direction of the incoming train. One of them wears a cassock.

Asher's heart is so lifted by this that he smiles. He walks back over to the lamp, extinguishes it, then steps back over to the open doorway, and waits patiently for his future to arrive at its own destination.

The train comes to a stop, with his car ending up about thirty feet beyond the assembled men. Asher steps out and walks back to meet them. The priest moves toward him, and Asher notices that he seems confused, and is looking at both Asher and at something behind him.

Asher stops and turns and sees that Cord Burnett has exited from one of the passenger cars. He cannot imagine how this could be. Burnett must have hidden himself somehow when they changed trains in Robstown. Asher notes that Burnett has replaced the Colt in his side holster.

For an instant, Asher thinks that Burnett is going to do something right then and right there. His face is flushed, and his anger and hatred are palpable. They regard each other for a moment, and then Asher turns back to the approaching priest, who has now figured out which one he is there to meet. They shake hands.

"I am Father Roberto Valdez," the priest says.

"I am Asher," Asher says.

Slowly, the men the priest has brought with him bring the casket off of the railroad car. Asher points to the stock car with the horse and pack mule and the old man's gear, and they are also unloaded onto the platform. The priest seems surprised by their presence but says nothing.

A station agent walks up to them from the inside, brisk and officious, and says, "That everything? We have a timetable here."

"No," Asher says, and points to the top of the car. All eyes turn upward, and they see polished wood overlapping the side of the car. The station agent sighs, and says, "Who the hell put that up there? Totally against the rules."

To Asher's surprise, the priest steps forward and quickly ascends the metal half-rings welded to the outside of the railcar that serve as a ladder. He gazes down at the recumbent crucifix, and he is so at a loss for words that he does not glance back down at Asher or any of the other men on the platform. He comes back down and looks at two of the men who came with him. "*Buscalo*," he says, pointing up, and the two men ascend the ladder, and stand on the top of the car. They, too, regard the crucifix for a moment, and then one of them pulls a knife from his belt and bends down to cut away the restraining cords holding it to the top of the car. When they have it free, they use the rope fragments to lower it carefully to the men below.

While this is happening, Asher regards Burnett, trying to get some sense of the man. After a moment, he walks over to him. Burnett is standing unsteadily on his feet, belligerent in demeanor and looking intently at Asher's face.

Asher wants some notion of what is happening, so he says, "Why don't you come with us?"

"Why don't you go straight to hell?" Burnett says. "Just go to hell. I'll be waiting right here when you come back."

Asher looks away, and down, and then back up. "I don't know how long I will be," he says. He walks back over to the priest, who has been watching this exchange. The priest is beginning to understand what is happening here.

The crucifix is down now, and Father Valdez turns to the station agent and says, "May we leave this here for just a few hours? I will send some men back for it."

The station agent purses his lips. "This ain't a church. Why would you want to leave this cross *here*?"

"It is a crucifix," the priest says. He motions to a windowless portion of the depot exterior. "Too big for us to carry. We will just lean it against the far wall over there. We will be back for it soon, I assure you."

"I can't guarantee someone won't steal it," the station agent says.

This strikes Father Valdez as amusing. "A fourteen-foot crucifix?"

The station agent shrugs, and says, "Suit yourself," and retreats into the depot. The priest turns to his men and points to the wall. "*Ponlo alli*," he says. Four of the men pick up the crucifix, and they take it to the wall. The crucifix is taller than the roof of the depot, so they carefully prop it lengthways along the wall, with the figure of Christ facing out.

The priest regards this for a moment and then says, "*Nuestro salvador está mirando hacia afuera. Víralo.*" The men move back toward the crucifix and have put their hands on it when something occurs to the priest, which Asher will only later understand. "*No te preocupes,*" he says, and the men move back away from it.

Asher has regarded this scene indifferently, so consumed is he with Burnett's intention. But now the men are surrounding the casket, and four of them pick it up heavily by the long brass handles that parallel both sides. The two others pick up the gear. Asher looks at the priest, who has taken the reins of the two animals. They begin to move down the length of the long platform, and Asher glances back at Burnett as they move away. Neither Burnett's posture nor position has changed.

It surprises Asher that there is no wagon waiting on the street, and he realizes that they are all going to walk across to the Mexican side. For several blocks, they move slowly down Elizabeth Street, wide and cobblestone-paved, with shuttered stores and shops on both sides. The men carrying the casket begin to breathe heavily in the brisk air under the strain. At East 13th Street they turn right and walk a block to the beginning of a wooden ramp, stepping over the train tracks in front of it. The structure's sole function is to take pedestrians down to the river without having to deal with the mud that results when the river rises. At the end of the ramp, quiet and eerie in the moonlight, a large, shallow ferry floats gently against the bank.

As they approach, an old man rises from a squatting position within the vessel and bends over to wrestle a heavy, thick plank from the floor of the ferry to the ramp. The plank is too narrow for the pallbearers to bear the casket into the ferry, so they set it down, and two of the men cross the narrow gangway to the ferry and turn to receive the casket, which has been laid on the plank. They pull the large box into the ferry, and then the other men enter the vessel, including the two with the old man's gear, and they pick up the casket and move it to the far side. Then Valdez hands the reins of the pack mule to Asher and leads the horse across the plank. Finally, Asher crosses with the mule, and the old man and one of the men pull the plank back into the ferry.

There are two cables crossing the river, about eight feet off the surface. The top of the ferry has a rope that is looped around one of the cables, to keep it in place against the flow of the river. The other cable is used to pull the ferry across, and Asher watches as the old ferryman rotates a large horizontal wheel, which slowly pulleys the large raft into motion. It is an exhausting effort, but a life of labor has muscled the old man, and the ferry slowly makes its way across the water.

The six pallbearers are resting now, all sitting on one end of the ferry, while Asher and the priest hold the leads of the two animals, watching the reflection of the full moon dance across the surface of the water. There is a very tranquil silence, except for the gentle lapping of the water against the sides of the vessel.

"So," Father Valdez says quietly, "what happened?"

There are many ways to answer this question, and Asher considers them, gauging each one by the effect it will have on the priest, and what direction the conversation could take from there.

"He was shot," Asher says finally, "by accident."

"Am I to understand that you are a Texas Ranger?"

Again, Asher reflects on this question for a moment and then says, "I don't know anymore. I honestly don't know."

The priest considers this and again imagines that he understands. "Did Emilio already have the crucifix when this happened?"

"No," Asher says. "He was on his way to San Diego when we came across him in the country. After he was dead, I found the telegram on him that you sent to Father Bard, so I went to San Diego to find out why he was headed there. When I figured it out, I just went ahead and brung it for him."

"Thank you," the priest says.

There is another leaden silence, and then the priest asks gently, "Was it you that shot him?"

And now Asher has to confront directly the question that has been poking at him for five days. He says nothing because the right way of saying it eludes him.

"Was he shot by the other gentleman we left behind at the depot?"

Asher is quiet again for a moment, and he finally surrenders to the right way of considering things. There must be, in *some* way, a shared responsibility by the group for the failure of an individual.

"We all did," Asher says.

The ferry sidles up to the Mexican side of the river, and they unload the casket and the animals and the gear, and a procession of sorts proceeds toward Matamoros, a half-mile distant, away from the river. They pass a dark and silent customs house, and twenty minutes later they enter the town. Their obvious destination is a large church, a cathedral really, moonlit and imposing in the cold night air. There is a post in front, where they tether the two animals, and then they proceed up several dozen magnificent steps and carry the casket through the heavy oak doors into the interior, through the vestibule, and into the sanctuary.

Asher is immediately overwhelmed with the vast space around him, dark and quiet, with islands of candles providing an illumination that feels timeless. It seems to Asher so somber that even the inevitable church mice must voluntarily take a vow of silence. A bier on wheels has been placed in the front, between the front row of pews and the massive communion rail that spans the entire width of the space. The priest leads the casket down the aisle and directs the six men to place it, *just so*, on the bier. That done, they all step back, breathing heavily, and kneel on the hard stone floor, and make the sign of the cross, and the priest prays aloud in Latin, which Asher recognizes from attending mass as a child with his mother. He removes his hat, and his thoughts during the prayer are a tangle of competing emotions.

At length, the priest finishes and the men cross themselves and get heavily to their feet. The priest dismisses them, and they file back out of the sanctuary, pausing to genuflect at the door to the vestibule.

Asher gazes around the sanctuary, at the wealth of statuary and murals, and a question occurs to him, and he asks softly, "Where will the cross go?"

"It's a crucifix," Father Valdez replies. "We have a side chapel with an exterior entrance. I can show it to you if you like."

Asher shakes his head. "No, thank you. I was just curious." Then, looking at the casket he asks, "When is the funeral?"

"Later this morning. Will you be staying?"

Asher looks at the priest and sees the fatigue etched into his face. The priest looks at Asher and sees that same thing.

"I can't," Asher says. "I need to get back. Me being here is probably a bad thing, anyway." Asher hesitates again and then says, "I don't want to leave right this minute, though, if you got something to say, or ask."

"Come to my office," the priest says, and he leads Asher to a small, cloistered room off the left side of the altar. It is the office of a busy man, with bookshelves dominating the back wall, and a desk in the center of the room, laden with open books and many loose papers. The priest motions Asher to a visitor's chair on the opposite side of the desk, and they sit.

"Will you tell me what happened?" the priest asks.

Asher answers immediately. "We was looking for someone else and stopped to question him. One of us shot him, completely by accident. We was miles from anywhere, and it was clear he was dying, and couldn't travel. The others went on, and I stayed with him."

"His death was hard?"

"I had some laudanum. I think that helped him some."

The priest senses the implication of this. "Your own laudanum?"

Asher looks down to the floor. "Don't put no virtue to it," he says. "We killed him. Ain't nothing trumps that."

"And so you helped him through, and then brought him back to us," the priest says. "Why? Why didn't you just bury your mistake? No one would have been the wiser. You have gone to much trouble."

"I got no words why it's been important to me," Asher says. "For the life of me."

"It is perhaps because of your sense of the *Imago Dei*," Valdez says.

"The what?"

Valdez regards Asher's fatigued and baffled face for a moment and then shrugs it all away. "It's not important," the priest says, because he knows that the *name* of a thing is of no consequence; it's the thing *itself* that matters. "Were you able to talk to him?"

"He didn't speak no English, and I don't speak no Spanish. But he did say something to me to give you. I wrote it down." Asher reaches into his shirt pocket and pulls out the reconstructed dictation. "I had to just write down the sound of the words he spoke. I hope this makes sense to you." He hands the pages over to the priest, who immediately begins to peruse them.

"For his wife, maybe?" Asher asks.

The priest does not look up from the papers. "He wasn't married. Actually, he was indigent. Very simple man. Drunkard."

"Why was he the one you sent for the crucifix?" Asher asks.

"Penance," Father Valdez says, again without looking up.

Asher is quiet for a moment until the silence becomes uncomfortable. He stands. "I should be going," he says.

"I think you should stay a little while," the priest says.

Asher goes cold inside. "Ain't nothing more I can do, or say," he says. "If you're going to file a complaint, on whichever side of the river, just tell me, and I will come back and tell whatever truth there is."

"No," the priest says, still regarding the paper in his hands. "It isn't that." He looks up at Asher. "Why don't you go back out and sit with Emilio, while I translate this formally?"

"Why?" Asher asks.

"Please," Father Valdez says. "Just for a little while."

Asher considers this for a moment and then nods, and walks out of the office, and goes back into the sanctuary. The priest returns his attention to Emilio Sanchez's words and pulls from a desk drawer several clean sheets of stationery. For the next thirty minutes, he attempts to put into intended Spanish what he sees in front of him. It is not an easy process. A word, phonetically written, occasionally makes no sense in context, even when he looks at it sideways in his mind, so he moves onto the next word or phrase. Then the necessary word will suddenly occur to him, and he will move back up and put it in. During this entire process, as the message slowly comes into focus for him, he feels an escalating sense of astonishment and wonder.

At length, he finishes it to his satisfaction, and takes a new piece of stationery, and translates the message cleanly to it, in English. When he is finished, he puts down the pen and prays.

Something wonderful is happening here, in this place, and it has been brought here by the exhausted, broken man sitting in the sanctuary. The priest cannot define or fully understand it, and he knows better than to try. For a moment, he feels jealousy at being only the conduit of what is being received, but he is a righteous man, and the feeling passes.

After a few moments, the priest goes to the door of his office that looks out into the vast spaces of the sanctuary, and he regards Asher for a moment, sitting quietly in the first row by the casket, eyes shut in either prayer or fatigue. He considers for a brief moment what he is about to do, and then he walks across the broad space between the altar rail and the front row of pews, pausing to genuflect as he crosses the aisle. As he approaches, Asher looks up at him with a weary curiosity.

The priest is holding a single piece of light blue stationery with a church letterhead. He has folded it, as though it is a formal letter, which, in a sense, it is. He holds it in his hands, hesitating.

"This is a most fascinating thing," he says. "Just remarkable."

Asher hesitates in turn and then asks, "What does it say?"

"He didn't speak these words to *me*," Father Valdez says. He hands Asher the letter and takes a step backward.

"He speaks them to *you*."

The priest returns to his office and stops again at the door and turns to regard Asher and stands transfixed as he watches him. Asher has pulled a pair of spectacles from his vest pocket, and he sits in the dim candlelight, head back, the page held up in his right hand while his left hand covers his left eye. Somehow, the image is one of great beauty to the priest. He sees Asher's gaze move slowly down the page, and as he approaches the end, the priest returns to his desk.

After a few moments, Asher comes to the door with the paper still unfolded in his hand, and he motions with it to the priest.

"He's saying things here that just don't make no sense," Asher says.

"He was dying. Great spiritual clarity can come at such a time."

"You said he was simple," Asher says. "These things ain't simple. He didn't know me. He's putting me in a place I just ain't seeing."

Father Valdez leans back in his chair, and Asher senses that the priest is threshing through this himself. "Who has paid for all this? For his casket? The crucifix? The money that I gave him wasn't enough."

Asher shrugs the question away. "That don't mean nothing."

"It means a great deal. I see your pain when you walk and when you sit. It is always there. How much of your laudanum did you share with him? All of it? Most? Who can say what God revealed to him in those last hours? Who can know the limitless ways that grace works?"

"I feel guilt, not pride," Asher says. "Good Lord, I helped kill him."

"You're thinking judicially," the priest says.

Asher considers this for a moment and says, "I don't understand."

How best to explain it to *this* particular man? The priest quietly sifts through his inventory of metaphors for the one most helpful, and then says, "The world is usually seen as evil, and the Church as a court-room, and Christ as the Judge. But it is so much *more*, Mister Asher. The world is sick, and the Church is a hospital, and Christ is the Great Physician. Not seeing it this way causes so much needless despair."

Asher is quiet again for a moment, and then he raises the paper again. "I got no idea what to do with this," he says.

"You must thank Almighty God for the glimpse of eternity that few of us are ever privileged to see. Graft it to your heart."

Asher regards him for a moment and then backs out of the door-way into the sanctuary, and the priest follows him to the pew with his gear. As Asher retrieves his coat and bag, the priest says, "Must you go?"

"Yes," Asher says. "My wife."

"Do you want me to send some men with you, back to the station?"

Asher considers this offer and then shakes his head. "No," he says, "but thank you. I've got to face him sooner or later."

"Farewell," the priest says, blessing Asher with a Sign of the Cross.

The streets of Matamoros, the walk to the ferry, where a different ferryman is waiting for him on the Mexican side, and then the trip back across the river all seem to Asher surreal. He can see the lights of the Brownsville depot on the bluff, and he thinks about the gun in his bag. He considers putting it on but then discards the idea.

They arrive on the Brownsville side, and Asher reaches into his pocket to pay the ferryman. The man wordlessly refuses it, and smiles, and says, "*Algo maravilloso está aqui.*"

"*No comprende,*" Asher says, but the ferryman has turned back to his wheel. Asher starts to speak again, but stops, not knowing what to say. He feels like the only man on God's earth that does not understand what is happening. He disembarks and walks slowly back to the depot.

When Asher arrives at the end of the platform, he stops and regards Burnett at the other end, sitting on the bench, facing the terminal, one leg out and one leg under. There is a bottle in his right hand. The light is bright and glaring, but Asher can discern nothing of Burnett's disposition. He knows that he could stand here forever and be no closer to knowing what to do. He prays for a moment, until he suddenly feels that he is just talking to himself. The course of what will happen, he realizes suddenly, isn't really up to *him*, but to Burnett. So he prays instead for Burnett and feels a sudden peace. And so steeled, he steps out onto the center of the platform and begins to walk to the other end.

At first, Burnett doesn't see or hear him, and Asher is afraid that when his approaching presence becomes obvious, Burnett will be startled into something reflexive and unthinking. He thinks of Sanchez's shooting. Burnett notices him, suddenly, and he stands up quickly and turns to him. His expression is completely impassive, and as Asher walks up to him, Burnett makes no move to touch the gun in his side holster.

"Hello, Cord," Asher says. "How are you holding up?"

For a moment, time and motion are suspended, and Asher readies himself for Burnett's fury. But then Asher sees Burnett's face go slack, and he knows now that there is no danger.

"I never meant to kill that man," Burnett says. "Honest to God. I never meant nothing like that to happen."

"Ain't anyone thinks otherwise," Asher says.

Burnett moves away and sits back heavily onto the bench, head down, the last of his fear and anger spent. He waves an empty whiskey bottle nonchalantly at the crucifix, with its suffering Christ. He says, "He's been staring at me all night," and now Asher understands the priest's desire to leave the crucifix behind, facing out. Burnett regards the bottle with indifference and puts it down on the bench beside him.

"Asher," he says, with a slow, slurred eloquence, "along with all else I done to that poor bastard, I stolt all his money at the undertaker. I have drunk and whored away every damn dime of it." Burnett turns and stares across the tracks at the sleepy cities on both sides of the river beyond, and Asher can see that this confession is coming at a great cost, at the end of a very great struggle. "I cain't make this right," Burnett says. "I cain't make *none* of this right."

"It's been covered," Asher says. He is looking at the crucifix.

The quiet of the night has descended on Asher now with an almost theatrical finality, and he gradually becomes aware, for the first time in many days, that he is waiting for nothing. All of creation seems to him in perfect harmony, in a pure, pulsating peace, and he is now being given a glimpse of many images attesting to something that he knows that he will never be able to comprehend fully: the clay of Emilio Sanchez lies in its beautiful box waiting for its piece of sanctified ground; the priest is moving slowly around the dimly lit cathedral, following the beautiful, white stations of the cross; Beulah lies in their bed, sleeping fitfully, praying when awake, waiting for his return; he imagines his brother's face softening when Asher will go to him after most of a lifetime, and embrace him, and repent; he imagines Horace Miller and Gerald Anspach, at peace with themselves finally, for making things right. He even imagines Render Moates, accepting his fallibility.

Asher sees these things, and he feels the trees, swaying gently in the pre-dawn breeze, and the serenity of the nascent morning air, and the cavernous silence of the depot, and even his own beating heart, as all *one thing* somehow, separate but connected, each at the center of circles that send out unfathomably beautiful ripples that cascade against each other and fold back into eternity. He knows that the intensity of what he feels cannot last, but that it will always hold fast in his soul in some measure. The voices in his dreams come to him: *Something wonderful is coming.* And then, a further notion: *Something wonderful is here.*

From beyond the city limits on the north side, the long, plaintive whistle of an incoming train drifts in, and he looks down at Burnett, and he is overcome with a feeling of deep kinship and sorrow for him. He puts his hand on the back of Burnett's neck and squeezes gently.

"Let's go home," Asher says.

Author's Note

While the overall political situation in the early spring of 1915,
as well as the Texas Rangers organizational structure,
is substantially as depicted here,
certain events and historical background detail
have been manipulated slightly in the interest of dramatic efficiency.
As an example, the Texas Rangers office in Laredo
had been relocated to Del Rio in the summer of 1914.
Neither was there yet, in March of 1915, a Company D.

Discussion of these and other changes,
and the reasons for them,
as well as a discussion of
the documentary sources used for this novel,
can be found in the relevant blog entries
on the Hymns of Kingdom website.

http://www.hymnsofkingdom.com

Acknowledgments

Whatever deficiencies this novel possesses, and there are many, it would have been exponentially worse had it not been for the dedicated squadron of advance readers who helped me at every stage of revision, beginning with the second draft. I will always be grateful to them for their candor and encouragement.

Ken Adcock
Sarah Aly
Dean Arnold
KB Ballentine
Ken Beecher
Dennis Bell
Lisa Bell
David Bird
Wayman Bolly
Nick Braker
Phil Brown
Terry Crisp
Aurelia and William Drake
James Drake
Beth Freeman
Hannah Freeman
Chris Greene
Nick Grisham
Mary Hamilton
Mary and Rodney Hartgraves
John Havener
Jane Hinman
Rachel and Chris Horton
Damaris and Joel Lajas
Al LaMontagne
Christian Leithart
Lawson Mabry

Wareen Mac Isaac
Barbara Martin
Emmett Martz
Edison McDaniels
Ellen Meyer
Maryann Miller
Thomas and Kristin Pope
Bonnie Presley
Brandy Reckley
Father Kevin Rigdon
Diane Rodriguez
Kayvon Sadrabadi
Stephen Sanders
Jim Stewart
Tommy Summers
Chuck Swafford
Dennis Thompson
Debra Church Tickel
Ethan Tickel
Kate Tickel
Mary Tickel
Tara Tickel
Greg Todd
Sam Tudisco
Susan Ward
Lyla Williams
Jan Worthington

Hymns of Kingdom

*In the immense cathedral which is the universe of God,
each man, whether scholar or manual laborer,
is called to act as the priest of his whole life –
to take all that is human,
and to turn it into an offering and a hymn of glory.*

Paul Evdokimov

www.hymnsofkingdom.com

Made in the USA
Columbia, SC
24 July 2022

63826871R10098